WILLIAM WENTON

AND THE
SECRET PORTAL

NORLA
NORWEGIAN LITERATURE ABROAD

This translation has been published with the financial
support of NORLA, Norwegian Literature Abroad

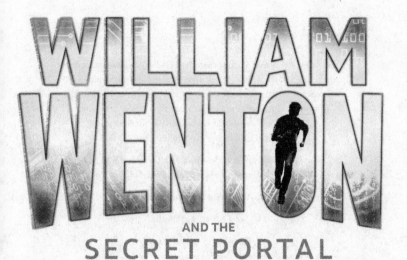

WILLIAM WENTON

AND THE
SECRET PORTAL

BOBBIE PEERS

Translated from Norwegian by
TARA CHACE

WALKER
BOOKS

First published in Great Britain 2018 by Walker Books Ltd
87 Vauxhall Walk, London SE11 5HJ

Published by agreement with Salomonsson Agency

2 4 6 8 10 9 7 5 3 1

Text © 2015 Bobbie Peers
Originally published as *Kryptalportalen* by Aschehoug
English translation © 2017 Tara Chace
Cover illustration by James Fraser

This book has been typeset in Adobe Garamond Pro

Printed and bound by CPI Group (UK) Ltd, Croydon CR0 4YY

British Library Cataloguing in Publication Data:
a catalogue record for this book is available from the British Library

ISBN 978-1-4063-7171-0

www.walker.co.uk

MIX
Paper from
responsible sources
FSC® C020471

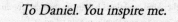

To Daniel. You inspire me.

Depository for Impossible Archaeology

Pontus Dippel positioned his forehead against the scanner next to the lift. He was on his way to do one last pass before he left for the night. The items downstairs, collected from all corners of the globe, were some of the rarest and most valuable artefacts in the world. Now they were safely stored in the Depository for Impossible Archaeology – a secured room beneath the Institute for Post-Human Research.

A green beam flashed across Pontus' forehead and the lift opened with a *ding*. He entered and two guard-bots wheeled in behind him as the doors closed. When the lift opened again, Pontus proceeded down a long hallway and stopped in front of a steel-clad security door. Neither Pontus nor the guard-bots noticed a dark figure materializing behind them.

Pontus placed his forehead on another scanner.

"Welcome," a computerized voice said.

The door slid open with a quiet *swish*, and light spilled

into the dark hallway. He was about to continue into the room when one of the guard-bots behind him said, "HALT!"

Pontus whipped around and spotted a figure coming towards them. A woman slowly stepped into the light. She had black, uncombed hair that draped like tentacles over her face, and rows of yellow teeth that snarled inside her grinning mouth. Something on the woman's left hand glinted in the dim light.

"HALT!" the guard-bot said again.

With one swift movement, the woman raised her metal hand and a beam shot out – vaporizing the two robots.

"No, it—it can't be…" Pontus said, holding up his hands in defence and backing away. "It's not possible. You're supposed to be … dead!"

The woman followed him into the room, closing the door behind them.

CHAPTER 1

William looked up at a red lamp in the ceiling that read: *live*. He could feel heat radiating from the powerful stage lights near by. A stressed-out woman wearing a headset stood across from him while busy workers passed around her, carrying large cables. William kept his gaze on the headset-woman. When she gave him the thumbs up, it would be his turn – his first appearance on TV.

Never in his wildest dreams had he imagined that he would find himself in a situation like this. William had lived under a secret name at an undisclosed address in Norway for most of his life, but now it felt as though everyone knew who he was – or at least had heard his name. And tonight, because he had solved the world's most difficult code, he was going to be on national TV. Slowly, he was being turned into a celebrity, and he wasn't sure if he liked it.

The woman with the headset gave him the thumbs up.

He heard applause from behind the stage wall and people calling him. There was something menacing about hundreds of people he didn't know shouting his name. William froze. It felt like his feet were stuck to the floor.

"William Wenton … where are you?" he heard the host's voice calling from the stage. "Maybe he found some code back there that he had to crack first."

The audience laughed.

Someone started chanting, "Will–yum … Will–yum."

Soon, hundreds of voices were chanting in unison, "WILL–YUM … WILL–YUM … WILL–YUM."

People clapped and stomped their feet. The headset-woman rushed over and angrily motioned for him to get going. William took a deep breath and slipped through the opening between two of the stage walls. He stopped as the bright lights hit his face – completely blinding him – and the audience burst into enthusiastic cheers.

"This way, William!" the host's voice said from somewhere in the light.

As William began to walk, he caught his foot on a wire and fell flat on his face. A few people gasped, but there was one person who laughed. It was Vektor Hansen, a self-professed genius and master code-breaker. The same self-professed genius William had beaten in solving the Impossible Puzzle, the world's most difficult code.

William kicked the wire away from his foot and stood up.

"I hope you're insured," the chubby host said, waddling over to help him up.

William looked up in confusion at Ludo Kläbbert, whose whitened teeth beamed in a broad grin. William hadn't seen Ludo since the Impossible Puzzle exhibition, where William had cracked a code that turned his life upside down. Ludo led William over to a sofa and gestured for him to sit.

Vektor stopped laughing the instant their eyes met and scooted over to put as much room between himself and William as he could, while Ludo slipped behind a desk and sat down. He smiled at them for a few seconds. William felt the heat from the broiling spotlights on the ceiling above and watched as two TV cameras rolled across the floor in front of them. One of the cameras pointed right at him and William could see himself on a screen at the side of the stage. He'd always had pale skin, but he looked extra washed-out now in the bright lights.

"So how does it feel, William … sitting here with the man you so epically humiliated a few months ago?" Ludo asked.

William had never tried to humiliate anyone. He looked at Vektor again, who had his arms and legs crossed – his loathing of the young code-breaker was very clear.

"How does it feel?" Ludo repeated impatiently.

"I don't know," William said. "I mean … I didn't mean to break the code."

"Didn't mean to break the code?" Vektor said, chuckling.

"How can someone solve a code that difficult without even wanting to?"

"Vektor has a point," Ludo said, looking at William. "How could you possibly have solved the Impossible Puzzle … by accident?"

William could have told them that forty-nine per cent of his body consisted of a high-tech metal called luridium – a metal that somehow allowed him to solve difficult codes in a trance-like state – but he stayed silent.

"He probably knew the solution beforehand," Vektor said, squinting at William.

"Is that true, William?" Ludo followed up. "Did you already know the answer?"

"No … I didn't know the answer," William said. He glanced out at the audience, who were sitting on the edge of their seats in rapt attention. "That's the truth. I didn't know anything. It just … happened."

They sat in icy silence for what seemed like for ever, then Ludo clapped his hands and grinned. "We can't get so carried away that we forget why we're really here." Ludo laughed, leaping out of his chair and pointing at the studio audience. "Are you ready to get started?"

The audience broke into rapturous applause.

"Are you ready for a challenge?" Ludo said, now pointing at William.

"Um…" William hesitated. No one had said anything

about a challenge.

"Great," Ludo cheered and snapped his chubby fingers in the air.

Suddenly, a woman in a long glittering dress appeared from behind the stage wall. She was pushing a serving trolley, with a big silver platter and a shiny lid covering it.

Ludo turned to the audience. "Are you ready?" he cried and pointed to the percussionist in the house orchestra beside the stage. An enthusiastic drumroll made the air in the hot studio vibrate and the audience started cheering again.

"What do you say," Ludo shouted to the crowd. "Should we give Vektor Hansen another shot?"

The audience responded with a "YESSS!" so loud that the floor trembled.

"Do you want to see what's underneath the lid?" Ludo pointed at the trolley.

"YEEEEEEAH!" the audience yelled, even louder.

With a dramatic gesture, Ludo grabbed the handle on the lid and whipped it off.

A gasp ran through the audience.

William couldn't believe his eyes. In front of him were two small colourful boxes. Both boxes had large gold letters on the front that read: *The Difficulty.* A plastic window underneath the letters revealed the contents: a metallic cylinder that looked like the Impossible Puzzle – the puzzle that William had once beaten Vektor in solving.

"Do you see what it looks like?" Ludo said, smiling at William. Ludo picked up a box so the audience could see it too. "These will be available in every toy store in the country tomorrow."

An excited gasp ran through the crowd. William couldn't believe it. It was a toy version of the Impossible Puzzle.

"Who wants two of the world's best code-breakers to compete to see who can solve the Difficulty the fastest?"

The audience burst into raucous applause. Did people really want the two of them to compete at solving a *toy*?

Ludo raised his hands to signal the crowd to be quiet, then he turned to William. "Well, what do you say, William? Are you ready for a challenge?"

William looked over at the audience and then at Vektor, who grinned at him, and William got the feeling that he had been tricked into this, and now, there was no way out.

"But they're not … real—" William started.

"Wonderful," Ludo cut him off. "And what do you say, Vektor?"

Vektor removed his leather waistcoat, and gave his blond ponytail a toss. "I'm always ready for a good puzzle." He cracked his fingers.

"The rules are simple," Ludo said. "The first one to solve the Difficulty is the winner."

Ludo nodded to the woman in the long dress. She opened the boxes and set both cylinders on the table in front of them.

Ludo raised his arms as if he were about to start a drag race, then he turned to William and Vektor.

"Are you ready?"

Vektor nodded.

Once again, William was about to protest, but he stopped himself. Yes, he had been tricked into this situation but he was in it now. In a split second, he adjusted his mind, looked at the puzzle in front of him and nodded. "I'm ready."

"GREAT!" Ludo shouted and started counting, "THREE … TWO…!" His chubby arms lingered for a couple of seconds, then dropped as he cried, "ONE!"

In a flash, Vektor snatched the cylinder. William did the same. He could tell right away that the toy wasn't the same quality as the Impossible Puzzle – most of the pieces were plastic and the device was a lot lighter. Sections of the cylinder could be turned and small square tiles could be moved up and down. Each square had a small symbol. William would have to move the pieces around in a specific order until he had solved the code.

He looked at Vektor, who was already well underway – his long fingers flying over the puzzle, twisting and turning the cylinder. Vektor was so engrossed in what he was doing that a drop of saliva had started to form on his lower lip.

William closed his eyes and concentrated, waiting for the luridium in his body to take over – the way it always did when he started to think about solving a code. Then he felt it. The unique sensation of the luridium starting to kick in – a tingling in his stomach that moved up his spine and out into his hands.

Everything around him disappeared and the cylinder began to glow and come apart – the various sections floating up into the air. William knew that only he could see the symbols as they twirled and looped above him. Some of them slid upwards, others sideways – a pattern was starting to form. This was how the luridium organized the codes so that William could calculate his own way to the answer. William looked down at the cylinder, and began moving the little squares around, mimicking the movements of the floating symbols.

Faster and faster his hands moved, twisting and turning the various sections of the cylinder at a breakneck pace. William knew that he was going to win – nothing could stop him now.

A bright light flashed in front of his eyes. At first, he thought someone had pointed one of the monstrous stage lights directly at him, but it felt like the light was inside his head – splitting into tiny lightning bolts that swam across his vision. A ringing in his head exploded like a bomb and he felt his body go limp. Something was wrong. His fingers were shaking uncontrollably – he could hardly hold on to the Difficulty, and the glow that had surrounded the puzzle an instant before was gone.

Something was *very* wrong. His whole body trembled and his hands were so cold that he could hardly feel them. Suddenly, William sensed that his surroundings had changed. Somehow, he was standing in a large cave. He looked up and saw an enormous glowing golden ring levitating in front of him.

And then, William was back in the studio. As if in slow motion, the cylinder slipped from his numb fingers, dropped to the floor and shattered. He stared in confusion at all the pieces lying on the ground in front of him. William saw people leaning over and whispering to each other, and then he looked up at Vektor, who was holding the two pieces of his toy up in triumph.

It had split in two. Vektor had solved it. He started hopping around like a deranged kangaroo, gloating, "I WON! I WON! I BEAT WILLIAM WENTON!"

CHAPTER 2

William sat at his desk looking down at the strange symbols on the surface of the metal cube that he was holding in his hands. William pushed one of the symbols and the cube made a loud *click* and started vibrating. He placed the cube on the desk – it was the last in a pile of other mechanical puzzles William had solved that night.

After his defeat on live TV, he had gone straight home and spent the rest of the evening completing one puzzle after the other without any problems. Most of the codes on the desk in front of him now were many times more difficult than that stupid toy. So what had happened at the studio? And what was that glowing ring he had seen?

He leaned back in his chair and looked out of the window into the dark night sky. He wondered what his grandfather was doing right now. Tobias Wenton worked for the Institute for Post-Human Research in England, and the last time William had seen him he was leaving on a secret trip – but that had been almost three months ago.

William opened a drawer in the large wooden desk that his grandfather had given him and lifted out a small metal crab, about the size of a dinner plate. The robot crab was part of a school assignment that his teacher, Mr Humburger had given him and William had been working on it for weeks now. The crab still needed a few minor adjustments so William grabbed a screwdriver and got to work.

A few hours later, William was sitting at the kitchen table. He hadn't slept a wink all night and his head felt like it was stuffed with cotton wool. His mum stood with her back to him, making pancakes – something she always did when William was feeling down. He looked over at a folded newspaper that was sitting on the table. The headline read: *William Wenton: Not so brilliant after all?* Underneath it was a picture of a euphoric Vektor Hansen, holding up his solved puzzle.

"Look … you can eat as many as you want," his mother said, setting a plate with a mountain of pancakes in front of him.

William shrugged. He didn't know what was worse: his defeat, in a competition everyone had expected him to win, or the sensation he'd had of losing control of his body. What was it that had come over him? Could it be some kind of seizure? He considered telling his mother, but she had been through enough these past few months, and he didn't want to worry her. He just had to hope that whatever it was wouldn't happen again.

His mother noticed the newspaper on the table. She snatched it away and stuffed it under a pile of old papers on the kitchen counter. Then, she turned to William and stood there watching him as he ate.

"Are you OK?" she said.

"Yeah," William lied. "Why?"

"It's just…" She paused, as if she wanted to plan her words carefully. "On TV… you seemed a little strange – like something was wrong."

"I'm OK Mum," William said and forced a smile.

His mother jumped as something crashed in the hallway. It sounded as if a piano had been dropped down the stairs. "He's starting to get the hang of it," she said, smiling. She seemed relieved to change the subject.

"Mhmm…" came a voice from the hallway.

Then they heard another bang followed by a loud crash and Mum hurried out.

"Do you need any help?" William shouted.

"Everything's fine!" Dad called back, followed by a couple of thumps and the sound of breaking glass. "It's a minor calibration issue."

"I never liked that vase anyway," William's mother said as she walked back into the kitchen.

William straightened up and looked towards the door. He could hear heavy footsteps approaching.

"Hi, William—" was all Dad managed before he continued at high speed into the kitchen. He had metal braces attached to the outside of his legs that ran all the way from his hips down to his feet. The braces were secured with Velcro straps at his ankles. "I can do this," he said, gritting his teeth as he staggered towards a chair like a toddler.

William's father was wearing a partial exoskeleton. William had watched a lot of nature programmes about animals with exoskeletons – like beetles – and he knew that the Greek word *exo* meant, "outside". The exoskeleton had been delivered by the Institute for Post-Human Research a few weeks before. The accompanying letter addressed to William's father, said that the exoskeleton was a new prototype they wanted him to test. It made it possible for people like William's father to get around without a wheelchair. This was the Institute's first prototype – an exoskeleton that would protect the wearer when they were searching in caves and jungles for hidden archaeological artefacts and ancient codes.

In the beginning he had flat out refused to accept the gift. After what William had gone through on his last visit to the Institute, his father didn't want anything to do with them but, in the end, William's mother had managed to convince him to give it a try. She might have been regretting that now – their house looked like a herd of buffalo had stormed through it.

William's dad stomped across the floor and crashed into the refrigerator. He tipped backwards, hitting the kitchen counter.

"How are you doing today?" he asked in a strained voice.

"OK," William lied again, putting a pancake on his plate.

His dad flopped onto the chair next to him. "Mmm, pancakes," he said, helping himself to three from the stack.

"Don't worry about what happened yesterday. We know you're the best code-breaker in the world," he said with a forced smile.

Hearing his father say those words helped. A year earlier, he had been so against William solving codes that he'd forbidden him from studying cryptology. But after the Institute had ultimately saved William from Abraham Talley, he had slowly warmed up to the fact that William had code-breaking in his blood – just like his grandfather. And right now, William felt good having someone who believed in him and backed him up, even if his father was wrong. William had lost fair and square at solving a toy puzzle – there was no escaping that – and his self-esteem had suffered a major blow.

Now he feared that the luridium that kept him alive and made him a codebreaking genius was malfunctioning. He had to get back to the Institute for Post-Human Research – he knew that only they could find out what was wrong with him.

CHAPTER 3

Mr Humburger stood in front of the class with his arms folded, staring at them with his cat-like eyes. William glanced at his teacher's sizeable belly, which jutted out at them. He could almost hear it counting down before it exploded and annihilated them all.

"Did everyone complete their assignment?" Mr Humburger said, scrunching up his eyes until they almost disappeared.

Twenty heads nodded in unison.

"William? Do you have anything to show us?" Mr Humburger said and gave him a cold stare. "Or have you been too busy making a fool of yourself on live TV?" He chuckled, a laugh that ended as abruptly as it had begun. Mr Humburger had never thought much of William – he didn't seem to like students who were smarter than him, and he definitely didn't like that William was now known as one of the world's best code-breakers. "Did you all get to see William's somewhat clumsy TV appearance?" he asked the whole class.

Everyone nodded again.

"Great," he chuckled, before heading towards William's desk. "I hope what happened has made you a little less interested in codes, and more set on making an effort at school?"

William didn't answer. He already felt quite defeated after what had happened on TV, but he couldn't show any signs of weakness in class. If he did, his teacher would use every opportunity to break him down even further.

"Have you brought in your assignment, William?" Mr Humburger asked.

William looked at his backpack on the floor. Of course he'd done his homework – the robotic crab was one of the coolest things that he'd made in a long time.

"Well?" Mr Humburger snapped, stopping in front of William's desk.

"He's brought something – it's in his backpack!" said a freckled girl who pointed at a thin metal leg that protruded from William's backpack. The leg jerked and wiggled. William started to regret bringing the crab to school – right now, he just wanted everyone to leave him alone.

"Well, let's see it then!"

A second leg appeared from William's backpack. It looked like the crab was trying to get out anyway, so he reached down, carefully scooped the little robot up and placed it on his desk.

"It's a prototype, and fragile—" William didn't have a chance to say any more before Mr Humburger grabbed the crab.

"Well, what have we here?" his teacher mumbled, holding the metallic crab up in front of his face for a closer inspection. "What does it do? Besides being some kind of mechanical crab-thing?" He knocked on the shell with his knuckles. The crab twitched and tried to wiggle free from his grip.

"Can I have it back now?" William asked. He didn't like the way Mr Humburger was handling the crab.

"Of course you can … after you've shown us what it does." Mr Humburger turned on his heels and returned to his desk.

William stood up and reluctantly walked to the front of the room. He picked up the crab and turned around to face the class.

"Sandy is a mechanical crab…" he began. "It can do several things, including walking, climbing and fetching things."

"Can it now?" Mr Humburger's chubby face contorted into a malicious grin. It was clear that he didn't have any faith in William's invention. "Show us, then."

William set the little crab down on the desk. It stood there without moving. William gave it a gentle nudge with his index finger, but nothing happened.

"Great work, William." Mr Humburger sneered.

A few of the students laughed quietly and a tall, thin boy – who happened to be Mr Humburger's favourite – snickered loudly. William wanted to grab the crab and run out of the room, but he didn't. Then its legs startled scuttling and the crab raced towards the edge of the desk. A gasp ran through the class.

"Catch it! It's going to fall," one of the girls yelped, but when the crab got to the edge of the desk, it stopped and changed direction.

"It knows when to turn around," William said to the class. Most of the students looked impressed now, and William felt a little better.

"What else can it do?" Mr Humburger asked, glancing at his watch. "Besides move its feet. Each presentation lasts three minutes, William; you have thirty-eight seconds left to show us something other than a wind-up toy."

"Sometimes it can climb up walls." William added.

"Sounds too good to be true," Mr Humburger said.

"It is true!" Now William wanted to show the class everything his crab could do. He set it on the floor and the crab shuffled sideways until it hit the wall at the other end of the room.

"Time's up," Mr Humburger said. "Collect the crab and return to your seat."

One of the girls pointed at the crab, which was already halfway up the wall. Tiny sparks flew off its metal legs as it moved upwards. William seized the moment.

"It has a static electricity generator in its belly," he explained.

"That's the same as when you rub a balloon against your hair and then it sticks to the wall."

The crab scrabbled up the wall until it reached the corner. It sat there for a little while before proceeding, upside down, across the ceiling.

"It hasn't done that before," William mumbled.

"What?" Mr Humburger said.

"That!" William pointed at the crab. "Walked upside down."

Everyone's eyes followed the mechanical crab as it darted back and forth on the ceiling until it suddenly crashed into a light and came to a halt directly over Mr Humburger. The light cracked and one of the crab's legs disappeared into the glass. William's heart almost stopped as sparks appeared inside the light and all the lights in the classroom blinked menacingly.

"Do something!" Mr Humburger shouted, pointing a chubby finger at William. "It's short-circuiting the whole school!"

William looked around. His eyes stopped on a long-handled broom in the corner of the room. He grabbed it and ran over to the crab. As William raised the broom, Mr Humburger yanked it from him and started swatting at the crab.

"It's stuck!" he shouted, hitting the crab even harder.

The crab fell from the ceiling and dropped onto Mr Humburger's head. The class gasped in surprise as the lights in the room blinked and died out.

"Get if off me!" Mr Humburger wailed, swatting at his head and tottering around in the semi-darkness. "Where is it?!"

"There it is!" one of the boys said, pointing at the crab, which lay on the floor behind the teacher. Smoke bellowed out from a crack in the metal shell.

"It's on fire!" Mr Humburger shouted and started whacking the crab with the bushy end of the broom.

"Stop!" William shouted.

But Mr Humburger didn't stop; he continued hitting the crab harder and harder.

William suddenly felt a stabbing pain in his head. A paralyzing cold spread through his arms as little dots of light appeared in front of his eyes. A high-pitched sound rang in his ears. He glanced down at his hands, which were trembling and as cold as ice. William's stomach lurched – this attack felt exactly like the one he'd had in the TV studio.

He had to get out of here. He tried to run, but he couldn't move. A bright light flashed across his vision and, for a brief moment, he was in the cave again, standing in front of the floating golden ring. Then he was back in the classroom.

William battled his way over to Mr Humburger, grabbed the crab and fled the room. He could hear his teacher shouting after him, but it sounded distant and scrambled – like William was underwater. The only thing that mattered now was to get away from everyone.

CHAPTER 4

William stopped on the pavement outside the school to catch his breath. The seizure seemed to have subsided and his hands had stopped shaking, but his heart was still chugging like a steam locomotive. What on earth was happening to him? He looked down at the robot crab in his hand. The smoke had ceased, but the little metal body was completely still. He placed the robot inside his jacket and started walking. He had to find someone who could help him.

"William…" a hoarse voice said. It was almost as if it had come from inside his head.

He stopped, and looked around. A dark figure was standing in the shadow of a bus stop just across the road. The figure stood so still that it almost merged into the background, but as it stepped forward William could see it was a woman with black shoulder-length hair that covered part of her face. She was wearing a black velvet jacket with metal buttons, a thick hood and long sleeves, and knee-high boots over her dark purple trousers. The woman's left hand was concealed by a black leather glove. William caught a faint whiff of something that smelled like burnt rubber and couldn't help but slightly recoil.

"You're trembling… Is everything OK?" the figure asked in perfect English. It still felt like the voice was somehow coming from inside William's head and he brought his hand to his ear.

"William," the woman continued. "Are you OK?" This time her voice came directly from her and William let go of his ear.

The figure took a couple of steps closer to William, who instinctively pulled back a little.

"Gotta go," he said as he started walking away.

"Wait," she said.

William sped up. Something told him that it was a good idea to get away from this woman as quickly as possible. He cast a quick glance behind him – the figure was gone, but he kept going. Then she was standing on the pavement about ten metres in front of him. He stood there bewildered. No one could run that fast – it was impossible.

"I need you to come with me, William," the woman said.

"Who are you?" William asked. His eyes scanned the surroundings for an escape route.

"You'll find out soon enough," she said and removed her leather glove to reveal a mechanical hand. It was like a robot's hand, made out of copper or brass – and it had blinking buttons, little gears and wheels, and a round pressure gauge on the wrist. The woman pushed one of the buttons – her mechanical fingers clicking as they moved – and the hand started to make a high-pitched sound.

"There's an easy or a hard way to do this. You decide," she said, pointing the device at William. "Either you come willingly or…"

William froze. What was she doing? Was her mechanical hand some kind of weapon?

"Defragging is quite painful," she said.

"Defragging?" William backed up into a lamp post behind him.

"Oh," the woman said, "it's the process by which I rip your atoms apart and turn you into a heap of dust. Of course, I can reassemble you again later … if I choose to."

The high-pitched sound grew louder and then a beam shot out from the woman's hand. William threw himself to the side and landed on his back in the middle of the street. To his horror, he saw that the lamp post was gone – like it had never been there at all. The woman opened a small lid in the mechanical hand, tilted it to the side and poured grey dust onto the pavement.

William got to his feet and started running. He had seen how fast the woman could move, and knew that he wouldn't be able to outrun her, but he had to try. Suddenly a black car came speeding up the street towards him. It screeched to a halt and the passenger door flew open.

"William, get in!"

He gasped. The man in the back seat of the car was his grandfather! William was about to jump in, when he stopped – Abraham Talley had once tricked him by shape-shifting into his grandfather. It seemed like Tobias knew what he was thinking and knocked on the window between him and the driver. The window lowered and one of the chauffeurs peered out at him. William recognized the highly advanced android that had saved him several times in the past. Reassured, he jumped into the back seat of the car, which accelerated the minute the door closed behind him.

William sat up in his seat and looked out of the rear window. The strange woman was gone.

"Are you OK? What were you running away from?" his grandfather asked.

"It was a woman – she just appeared from nowhere," William said breathlessly. "She shot at me!"

"Shot at you?" his grandfather asked. "With what?"

"She had some kind of mechanical hand," William said. "It fired rays that made stuff, well … disappear."

The colour in his grandfather's face started to drain away and William shifted in his seat uncomfortably. "Did she say anything to you?" Tobias asked slowly.

"She wanted me to go with her," William said. It wasn't until now that he felt his body shaking from adrenaline. He took a deep breath and tried to relax.

"Good thing we came when we did then," his grandfather said and forced a smile.

"Do you know who she is?"

"No," his grandfather said and paused. "Not yet … but I saw what happened on TV yesterday." William got the feeling his grandfather was holding out on something, but then again so was he. He had been foolish to think his grandfather, right along with the rest of Norway, hadn't seen William freeze.

"I don't know what happened. It was as if—"

"As if you lost control of your body?"

"Yes." William nodded and looked down at his hands. "How did you know that?"

"It's just a theory – we'll have to run some tests on you to find out exactly what it is though." His grandfather paused again. "Are you ready to come back to the Institute?"

"Yes," William nodded.

"Great." Tobias smiled and tousled his hair. "I thought you would. We'll message your parents on the way so that they know where you're going." He cast a quick glance out of the rear window, then turned and knocked on the glass between them and the android. The car suddenly changed direction and accelerated.

CHAPTER 5

The car pulled up outside the gates of the Institute for Post-Human Research. Only a few hours before, William and his grandfather had been driven to a secret airfield not far from William's home in Norway. The car had then been loaded onto a hi-tech plane, which had taken them to England, and on to the Institute.

"After Abraham Talley was placed in the basement, we had to raise the security level," William's grandfather said, pointing at the two guard-bots stationed at the gates.

William shuddered. Abraham Talley had tried to kill William before the Institute had captured him – freezing Talley in an escape-proof container and locking him away in one of their secure rooms.

A guard-bot wheeled towards them and stopped next to the car. It looked like a fire hydrant on wheels. The robot had two arms and one large eye at the top of its head, which could

34

rotate 360 degrees like an owl. At the Institute, guard-bots were known for their stubborn single-mindedness – not their people skills. William's grandfather lowered the electric window and peered out.

"Identification scan," the guard-bot said, raising a rectangular screen.

"Certainly," William's grandfather said and stuck his head out of the window.

The guard-bot placed the scanner up to his forehead and pressed a button. The scanner hummed for a bit, then a light on top of it blinked red a couple of times before turning green.

"Tobias Wenton. Clear," the guard-bot said.

"Your turn." William's grandfather motioned for him to do the same. "It scans your brain, which is the most accurate form of identification."

The screen turned green again and the car continued through the gates down a long, gravel road that led to the main building. A large lawn stretched out on both sides with only guard-bots patrolling the area.

"Where are all the people?" William asked.

"We've had to send the vast majority home," Tobias said. "The Institute is more like a high-security prison now than an advanced research facility."

"Because of Abraham?" William asked.

"More or less." Tobias seemed far from pleased.

The car stopped in front of the main doors and William

looked up at the stone building looming above them. Even though it was only a little more than four months ago, it felt like for ever since he was last here and he was excited to be back. William opened the door and went to jump out, then he felt his grandfather's hand on his arm.

"William," he said. "I'm not staying."

"What?"

"I have to get going right away," Tobias continued. "There's urgent business I need to take care of."

"Urgent?" William said.

His grandfather paused and looked steadily at him. "There's been an incident here at the Institute … something's gone missing, and I'm going to try to get it back."

"What's gone missing?" William said.

"Nothing you need to worry about," Tobias said. "You have your own problems to sort out."

William couldn't believe it. He had been really looking forward to spending some time with his grandfather and it seemed ridiculous that he was leaving so suddenly when he didn't yet know what was even wrong with William.

"I'm sorry," his grandfather said gently. "I wish I could stay here and explain, but the most important thing right now is that the Institute run tests on you straight away to find out what's causing your seizures. You'll be safe here – I've asked Benjamin Slapperton and Fritz Goffman to look after you."

William sat back in his seat. He thought about everything that had happened – his seizures, the strange woman who had attacked him, the heightened security at the Institute and his grandfather's haste to leave. Somehow, all of these things were connected; he just didn't know how.

"That woman outside school," William said. "How does she fit in to all this?"

"We're not sure yet, but we'll let you know as soon as we find out." Tobias pointed at something behind William. "There he is now."

William turned and saw Benjamin Slapperton coming out of the building. He seemed nervous and his eyes scanned the surroundings before he waved at William and quickly disappeared back inside.

"You'd better get a move on," his grandfather said and smiled reassuringly.

William got out of the car and watched it speed away down the gravel road. He hurried up the stairs and stepped inside the enormous hall. Slapperton was waiting next to something that looked like a hovering golf cart, with a large fan secured behind two black rubber seats.

"Finally," Slapperton said, jumping into the driver's seat and patting the cushion beside him. "We don't have much time – get in and put your seatbelt on." He pushed a button on the dashboard and the fan whirred into life.

*   *   *

As they zoomed down the hallway, William looked up at Slapperton. He was happy to see his old teacher again – his hair fluttering in the airstream from the fan and his glasses bouncing up and down on his nose. In spite of the strap holding him in, William almost fell off as Slapperton jerked the steering wheel to the left – bumping the cart into the wall as it swerved sideways into a corridor and continued on even faster. William held on to the seat with both hands.

"Why are we in such a hurry?" he said over the noise from the fan.

"Look around." Slapperton pointed with one hand. "The Institute is not the same."

"All because of Abraham?"

"Exactly," Slapperton replied. "Nothing can be done around here any more. I only leave my lab when it's absolutely necessary."

"But why all the security?" William asked. "He's frozen. It's not like he's going to get up and leave."

"This is Abraham Talley we're talking about. We can't be too careful. Besides, the security is as much about keeping anyone from getting in as it is about keeping him from getting out."

"People getting in … to rescue him?" William asked.

"It's just a precaution really," Slapperton said. "We think all the followers who used to help him out are long dead – one of the downsides of Talley being semi-immortal, I guess."

Suddenly Slapperton hit the brakes so hard that William

was flung forward in his seat. He gestured at two guard-bots standing in front of a barrier blocking the hallway. One of the robots rolled up to their cart.

"We did all this four minutes ago." Slapperton seemed irritated.

The guard-bot didn't respond and held up the same kind of scanner that William had gone through at the first set of gates. After they had both passed the scan, the guard-bot pressed a button on the wall. The gate swung out and slammed into the wall with a metallic clank. Slapperton stepped on the pedal and the hover-cart moved forwards again.

"No one's allowed to travel in the hallways without clearance. And anyone under the age of eighteen needs to be accompanied," Slapperton said.

"So how am I supposed to get around?" William asked.

"We'd prefer it if you didn't," Slapperton said and turned the wheel again.

They swerved around a corner and grazed a red robot that looked like a large fizzy drinks can on wheels, with one large eye that rotated around the rim at the top.

"But if you must get to somewhere alone," Slapperton said, pointing at the robot they'd almost run over. "You use one of those."

"Look where you're going!" the robot shouted after them.

"That was a porter-bot. They're all over the Institute. You hail one and it will come, like a taxi. Or you can order one from your room when you want to go out – your door will arrange it."

A couple of guard-bots stopped and looked at William as the cart passed. These robots carried laser-like guns.

"What are those weapons?" William asked.

"Passivators," Slapperton said. "They shoot rays that make the atoms in your body unstable – nasty things. They work on machines too. We call it jelly-technology for lack of a more sophisticated word."

"What happens if you get shot with one?" William asked.

"Your body becomes wobbly like jelly. Stay away from them."

"Is Iscia still here?" William asked. He'd been looking forward to seeing his friend again, but now he was afraid that she was gone.

"She's one of the few left," Slapperton said. "She's a Field Agent now."

William felt a surge of relief – he couldn't wait to see her again.

"What's a Field Agent?" William asked.

"She's no longer a candidate – she has real duties now." Once again Slapperton turned the wheel and they swerved into another hallway. "Here we are," he announced as they stopped next to a metal door.

William read the sign on the door: *Ultrasonic Lab*. Slapperton hopped out of the hover-cart and checked from side to side like a scared field mouse. He entered a code on the control panel next to the door, which emitted a brief *bleep*.

"In we go," he said, waving to William and opening the door. "This is where the magic happens."

CHAPTER 6

Slapperton seemed to relax a little more inside the lab, but not before he'd secured all eight of the locks on the inside of the door and bolted it with an iron bar. Then he turned to William and looked at him properly for the first time.

"You've changed," he said. "Grown taller… How long has it been since you were last here? A few months?"

"Four months and thirteen days," William said. He'd counted every single day. "I hoped I'd be able to come back sooner though."

"I understand, but we couldn't bring you back until it was absolutely necessary."

"And now it is?" William asked.

"Yes – you could put it that way," Slapperton said. "We've been paying you special attention."

"Why?" The thought of someone spying on him didn't sit well.

"Your grandfather knew the risks when he injected you with luridium. We need to keep track of the luridium in your body." He watched William for a moment before clapping his hands. "Anyway, I want to show you something. Follow me!"

William followed Slapperton further into the lab. Amidst all the instruments, he could see a steel-framed glass tank that stood on a table. Inside the tank sat a medium-sized cockroach. It was waving its antennas around and moved a little closer to the window as if it realized they were there. It seemed to be looking right at them.

"We found it in the flooded bunker after the incident in London," Slapperton said. "After the water from the Thames broke through, we had to use submarines to explore the area. We discovered a large network of passageways down there."

William shuddered, remembering what had happened in the bunker in London. It had been four months, but now it all came back to him: the dark, endless tunnels; the big door that only opened with the right code and the cavernous hall with the submarines and military vehicles. Then there was the cryogenic storage container where he'd found Abraham Talley – the same Abraham Talley who was now lying frozen solid down in the Institute's basement.

"We found the cockroach in one of the air pockets," Slapperton said. "As a matter of course we brought it back here to study it, the way we do with everything we find down there, and…" He stopped, and stood there watching the cockroach.

"And?" William said.

"In a way, you and that cockroach are in the same boat, because of what you have inside you."

William stared at him. "You mean the luridium?" he asked.

"It doesn't have much inside it, but if you were to touch it, the luridium inside of you – being a larger amount – would pull the luridium out of the cockroach … and into you."

"Like Abraham tried to do to me in London," William added.

"Correct," Slapperton said. "And the funny thing is that the roach has exactly enough luridium inside of it to make you fifty–fifty … exactly half human, half machine."

"What would happen to me then?" William said, studying the tiny insect.

"Your abilities would increase," Slapperton said. "But at a great risk… You could tip over … and become more machine than human."

"Is that what happened to Abraham Talley?" William asked. "He tipped over?"

"Yes. He lost the human in him completely."

William looked at the cockroach. Was it really possible for him to become a machine? Up until now, William had thought of the luridium inside of him as a blessing – after all, it had kept him alive when he had suffered a spinal injury as a child. But the thought that the same intelligent metal that had saved him could also cause him to lose his human qualities was devastating. It felt like he had an enemy inside of him – an enemy he could never get rid of.

"How did it get the luridium?" William asked, peering at the cockroach behind the glass.

Slapperton shrugged. "We don't know. Luridium is very rare."

"Why are you keeping it locked up like that?" William asked.

"We're running tests on it…" Slapperton paused for a bit. "They were going well – up until yesterday."

William thought it over. Then it hit him.

"You mean when I was on the TV show?"

"Exactly," Slapperton said. "We saw what happened to you. You had a seizure at the same time the cockroach did." He was talking faster now. "The cockroach started trembling just as you did, and its body temperature plummeted."

He looked at William to see how he would react.

"So…" Slapperton started, but stopped, as if he were having trouble figuring out what he wanted to say.

"If we both had attacks," William said slowly, "then it must have something to do with the luridium?"

"Yes," Slapperton said. "And I think I know what caused it – I just don't know where it came from yet."

"Where what came from?" William asked quietly.

"Sound waves," Slapperton said, his voice trembling with excitement. "Watch this."

He pushed a couple of buttons on a control panel next to the window. The cockroach started vibrating and then flew at them, crashing into the glass.

William backed away and stopped. He stood there watching the insect thump its head into the pane of glass. Then it did a backward somersault and hit the wall before racing around in a circle. It looked like it was trying to break out of the container. Slapperton pushed the button again and the vibrations stopped. The cockroach lay lifeless for a few seconds, then shook itself off a little and got back up.

"What did you do?" William said, without taking his eyes off the cockroach.

"I recreated the high frequency of the sound waves that must have somehow triggered your attack."

"But why didn't anything happen to me?" William asked.

"The cockroach is behind reinforced soundproof glass," Slapperton replied and rapped on the glass. Then he faced William. "And now, it's your turn."

CHAPTER 7

"I have to run some experiments before I know if I can help you or not," Slapperton said as he walked William over to a strange-looking chair in the middle of the room. It reminded William of a dentist's chair, surrounded by various weird instruments. He'd never been a big fan of the dentist, and after what had happened to the cockroach, he now wasn't a fan of sound waves either. He glanced up at some kind of laser cannon mounted on the ceiling above the chair.

"What's that?" he asked.

"Relax," Slapperton said with a smile. "It's not as dangerous as it looks. I call it a particle frequency manipulator. It's going to send high-frequency sound waves into you," he said simply, and started tinkering with the cannon.

"Like the cockroach?"

Slapperton nodded. "By the way," he said, changing the subject, "I want you to forget about what happened on TV – that

Vektor guy is a big show-off … he has nothing on you."

William smiled and relaxed a little.

"When I got back to my lab after the TV show," Slapperton said and pointed at a large box in a corner, "I noticed that the audiometer over there had short-circuited."

"What's an audiometer?" William asked.

"It's like a seismometer that's used to register earthquakes – only the audiometer measures sound waves that are inaudible to the human ear." Slapperton hesitated and stared at it for a few seconds. "The audiometer works twenty-four seven, constantly monitoring the airwaves. During the TV show, it registered sound frequencies so high that the audiometer stopped working, but I quickly calculated the frequency that caused it, and programmed it into the cannon."

"So, you're going to make me have another attack with that cannon?" William asked. He already knew the answer, and he didn't like it.

"William, this attack… When you lose control of your body and your mind, you become a threat not only to yourself, but to everyone around you. You saw what happened to the cockroach."

William gulped. Could he be dangerous? Was he capable of hurting someone – even if he didn't have control over it? He turned and sat in the strange chair, looking up at the cannon, which was pointed right at him. Slapperton pressed a few buttons on a control panel and it started humming.

"Could you place your arms there?" he asked, pointing

to the armrests on either side. "I have to strap you in… It's for your own safety. I've done this many times before on the cockroach, and it's been completely fine. I'll start out gently and then increase the waves, little by little."

Slapperton pushed a button on the side of the chair and the seat back started vibrating. "Are you ready?"

William nodded. "Ready."

He took out a pair of ear defenders and placed them on William's head. He then sat behind a screen and put on a huge helmet and a heavy jacket with a badge on the arm that read: *protective lead wear.*

Not dangerous? William thought. *Nothing to worry about?* It looked like Slapperton was about to detonate a nuclear bomb. He pulled a lever and the cannon began to hum. William grabbed the armrests and squeezed his eyes shut. He didn't feel anything at first – he could just hear the loud humming sound from the cannon over him and now understood why he had to wear ear protection. The vibrations travelled through his body in waves, making him feel like he was slowly disintegrating. The noise moved into his head and the vibrations spread down his spine. William opened his eyes and looked at Slapperton.

"What's happening?" he shouted.

But Slapperton was too busy fiddling with the control panel to hear him.

William felt a stinging pain in his head. Then he heard a high-pitched sound. The pain increased until it felt like his brain was going to explode. He opened his mouth to yell to Slapperton, but he couldn't make a sound – it was as if he'd lost control of his own body.

A terrible cold spread all the way out to his hands, like the last times he'd had an attack, then a violent jolt travelled through him. Suddenly, everything around him was gone and all he could see was a bright light. He blinked – desperately trying to focus his eyes – then he spotted something way down below ... it was an enormous mountain range. With a sickening feeling, William realized that he was floating high up in the air, in the middle of a blizzard.

He started to panic, then, without warning, he plunged towards the mountains at tremendous speed. He was going to crash right into the tallest mountain peak. William closed his eyes and waited for the impact.

When he opened his eyes again, he was standing inside a huge cave with grey stone walls. A large sparkling ring hovered in the middle of the hall – the same golden ring he had seen during his first attack. Then he spotted something on the ground below the golden ring. It looked like a white coffin, on wheels. William had never seen it before, yet somehow he felt he should know what it was.

Before he could get any closer, a blinding white light flashed in front of his eyes. William looked around. He was back in his chair. Slapperton ripped off his protective gear and ran over to him.

"Stay still," he said, peering into William's ear with a little otoscope. "Open wide." William opened his mouth and Slapperton shone a torch into his mouth. "Looks normal," he mumbled and made a note on his notepad. "How do you feel?"

William was shaken and confused. He felt like he'd travelled out of his body, but he had no idea how he could have. Could the mountains and the strange golden ring be something that his brain had somehow made up?

"What happened?" William asked.

"You tell me," Slapperton said as he undid the straps around William's arms. "What did you see?"

"A bright light," William said. "And then I was way up in the air."

"Yes…? Yes?" Slapperton exclaimed. "And?"

"I saw mountains."

"Mountains?" Slapperton said, straightening up. He stared at William as if he didn't quite believe him. "What kind of mountains?"

"Really big ones, maybe the Himalayas," William replied and looked up at Slapperton, who looked terrified.

"The Himalayas… Are you sure?" he asked, his voice shaking.

"I don't know," William said. "Pretty sure…"

"Did you see anything else?" Slapperton leaned in closer.

"I saw a big room deep down inside a cave…"

"Go on!"

"And a kind of floating hoop … like a huge golden ring. And a white box underneath it."

Slapperton stood there, staring at William.

"What does it mean?" William asked.

"I don't know… But it's not good," Slapperton said. "It's not good at all."

CHAPTER 8

The hover-cart came to a sudden halt as it bumped into the wall next to William's room.

"We'll do some more, less painful, tests tomorrow." Slapperton clutched the steering wheel and scanned the hallway with worried eyes.

"OK," William said and climbed out of his seat. Although the ordeal had been unpleasant, William felt fine now and he was really looking forward to being back in his old room again.

"I have to make sure you get safely inside your room," Slapperton said, tapping his fingers on the steering wheel as he waited for William to open the door. "I'll pick you up tomorrow," he shouted as the large fan behind him hummed into life again. "And William…"

"Yes?" William shouted back.

"It's very important that you don't solve any codes while

we're trying to figure out what's causing your attacks, OK? We don't want to set off an attack accidentally."

William nodded and stepped through the door. Finally, he was back, but something was different. The bed and desk had been bolted to the floor and the walls were covered with thick steel plates. Daylight seeped into the room through the metal bars outside the little window. It looked like a prison cell.

"Welcome, William," the door said as it closed with a *click* behind him.

"Door?" William said, as he turned to look at the door. He smiled as he remembered how alarmed he had been when he first met the talking door.

"Same old door! Would you like a cupcake?" the door asked. A hatch opened in the door and a long arm shot out. It stopped right in front of William's face with a fresh cupcake on a plate, still warm from the oven.

"Cool, huh?" the door said. "I got a new arm! It's much more practical. Now I can finally bake."

But cupcakes were the furthest thing from William's mind right now. "What happened to my room?" he asked.

"Do you want the cupcake or not?" The mechanical arm extended even further, like a telescope, shoving the cake in William's face.

"No thanks." William pushed the cupcake away.

"It's called the Isolator," the door said, sounding a little disappointed.

"The Isolator?" William said.

"Yes, that's what they call it, when a room is secured this way. You could explode a bomb in here without anyone hearing it."

"It looks like a holding cell," William said as he walked over to the window. He could hardly believe what he saw through the metal bars. A tall white wall that was almost as high as the trees extended all the way around the enormous grounds. Guard-bots with passivators patrolled along the wall that was dotted with giant watchtowers and enormous spotlights mounted on top.

"If you're thinking things are worse than the last time you were here, then you're wrong," the door said. "It's actually much worse… That's why I've taken up baking – to lighten things up a little. It's getting cold." The arm held out the cupcake again.

"All of this because of a frozen old man in the basement?" William said, trying to ignore the cupcake hovering in front of his face.

"Not just any old man," the door said. "He has the potential for great destruction in him."

William fell silent and looked at his hands. The luridium – the very thing that made Abraham Talley so dangerous was what William had inside of him. He felt more like a freak than ever before.

"Oh, I'm sorry," the door said. "I didn't mean to—"

"It's OK," William said. "I'll take that cupcake now." He

hoped the sugar would perk him up a bit. He took a bite – it was delicious.

"Anyway, it was only very recently that the security was upped to Level Five," the door said matter-of-factly.

"Really? I assumed it had changed when Abraham came to the Institute. What happened?" William asked with his mouth full of cake.

"I'm not supposed to tell you," the door said.

"But you just did," William said and swallowed. "And it would make me feel a lot better if you told me more."

The door was silent for a few seconds before carrying on. "When Abraham arrived here, the security level was raised to Three. Then something happened in the Depository yesterday, and they raised it all the way to Level Five."

"The Depository?" he said. "What's the Depository?"

"Never mind," the door said.

"What happened there?" William asked.

"Nothing," the door said. "Would you like another cupcake?" The hatch opened and the mechanical arm shot out and held the cupcake right in front of William's face. "This one has a hint of vanilla."

William pushed the arm away. "I want to know what happened in the Depository. If something strange is going on, I need to find out what it is. It might be related to what's happening to me."

"All I can say is that something happened in the Depository

for Impossible Archaeology … and after that, they moved something from the Depository to one of the sonic labs in the basement. I'm sorry, but I really can't tell you any more – if they find out I've said anything, they'll give me refrigerator duty for the rest of my life."

William knew that he wouldn't get any more information out of the door, but he was sure that something strange was going on at the Institute and he needed to find out what it was. The basement seemed like a good place to start.

"I need some fresh air," William said. "Could you order me one of those porter-bots?"

"Now?" the door said with hesitation in its voice.

"Yes, now!" William said.

The door was silent for a little bit. "It's a little late," the door said. "But maybe I can get hold of one… If you'll try another cupcake."

CHAPTER 9

A few minutes later, William was walking briskly down the hallway. He took a bite of his second cupcake and the taste of vanilla flooded his mouth – the door really knew how to bake. A porter-bot wheeled in front of him. William had told the robot that he had dropped something outside Slapperton's laboratory, and now they were headed downstairs to find it. William didn't like lying – not even to a robot – but he had to find out what was going on at the Institute.

"We need to hurry," the porter-bot said, turning a corner and speeding up. "I'm picking someone else up in four minutes and thirty-eight seconds. I'm on my third triple shift this week and I'm running low on oil and electrolytes. No time to recharge."

William jogged to catch up with the stressed-out bot. "I'm sure I can find my own way down there," he said.

"Anyone under eighteen is forbidden to move around the

Institute alone." The porter-bot accelerated even more.

"But isn't that just a precaution? Surely there's no real danger around here?"

William knew that there was a good reason for the heightened security, but he was fishing to see what the porter-bot knew. Sometimes robots blurted out stuff they weren't supposed to say.

"Danger?" the porter-bot said. "Right now, there's more danger than ever. It's so bad that some of the porter-bots refuse to work alone. You've probably seen them roaming around in groups, following each other."

"Why is it so dangerous?" William asked, now running to keep up with the robot.

"Don't know," the porter-bot said. "Our orders are to be on the lookout for things out of the ordinary."

"What kind of things?" William said. This robot clearly knew a lot more than it was letting on.

"Anything that's not supposed to be here," the porter-bot said and sped up.

"Anything?" William asked. "What do you mean?"

"We don't have much time. We need to take a shortcut." The robot abruptly turned into a narrower hallway and headed for the stairs at the other end. William ran after it.

"But—" William protested.

"This route is thirty-eight seconds faster," said the porter-bot. William stopped and watched as the robot clanked down the stairs like an out-of-control dustbin. Finally, it landed on the floor at the bottom.

"Hurry up!" it said as it whizzed off down the hallway.

William hesitated. He sensed that it was dangerous to keep going – but his curiosity about the secret room was stronger than his fear. He hurried down the stairs to find the porter-bot waiting for him in front of a lift door at the other end of the hallway.

"Come on," it said and waved. "We have to get a move on!" The robot raised its hand up to a sensor on the wall next to the door.

"Authorized," the door said, and opened. William followed the robot into the lift and the door closed.

"Level 2A," the porter-bot said.

"Level 2A coming up," the lift said and, with a jolt, started its descent.

William looked at the porter-bot's hand. He thought back to the orbs the Institute had given all the candidates the first time William had come here. The orbs were puzzles to be solved, and for every new level they reached, they were given access to new parts of the Institute.

"Do you have access to the whole Institute?" William asked.

"More or less… Why?" The robot eyed him suspiciously.

"Just making conversation," William said.

"There are places I can't go," said the robot. "Because of heightened security levels."

"Ah yes, the door was telling me…" William started.

"So restricted areas like 1A—" the robot blurted out, but stopped itself.

"1A?" William said, looking at the porter-bot. "What's 1A?"

"Nothing… It's extremely restricted!"

"Level 2A," the lift said, followed by a soft *ding* as the doors opened.

"Come on!" The porter-bot shot out of the lift.

But William didn't move. He knew that this might be his best chance to find the secret room. He watched as the porter-bot continued down the hallway – it was in such a hurry it didn't even notice that William was still inside the lift.

The doors closed shut in front of him.

"Level 1A," William said.

"Level 1A coming up," the lift said.

When the doors opened again, William quickly jumped out and peered into the hallway in front of him. It looked the same as the one he had just left, but it was much darker and ended in an L-junction about twenty metres further down. A sign on the wall read: *Highly restricted area. Keep out!*

William didn't want to be down here any longer than necessary – especially as the porter-bot had said that everyone was on the lookout for something that didn't belong. William caught himself wishing that he had gone to find Iscia before he had started exploring, but it was too late now. He slowed as he got closer to the end of the hallway, then he stopped and listened. Nothing.

He sneaked up and peeked around the corner. Another sign on the wall read: *Forbidden. No entry!* Two cameras – one in each corner – watched a set of heavy iron doors. The camera rotated to face William – the guard-bots would soon be on their way. But William had already crossed the point of no return. He was determined to continue and see how far he could get before they stopped him.

William turned his attention to an advanced control panel on the wall. He knew that he would have to hack his way into the system to override the panel and open the door. He was sure he could do it; he just hoped that it wouldn't trigger another attack like Slapperton said it might.

He took a deep breath and leaned in towards the panel – focusing his gaze on it. William immediately felt vibrations in his stomach. He tried not to think about being apprehended by guard-bots with passivators and instead stared at the digits and letters on the control panel. The vibrations moved up his spine and out into his arms and fingers. Then, as it always did, everything around him seemed to vanish and all he could see was the control panel.

One digit after the other started lighting up – blinking like disco lights. At first, it seemed random, but then a pattern emerged. William knew that the luridium in his body was helping his brain to find the solution and his fingers started working immediately, pressing the buttons one after the other as they lit up. The flashing lights blinked so fast now William had a hard time keeping up. This code was a tough one.

His fingers stopped. William straightened up, rubbing his sore hands as he looked at the panel. Had it worked? The control panel flashed a couple of times, gave a quick *beep* and the heavy iron doors opened.

William looked back; he was still alone in the hallway. He slipped inside and the door closed behind him.

CHAPTER 10

William found himself in a room that looked like an enormous space station. The walls and ceiling were covered with golden metal panels and a symphony of bleeps and hums came at him from rows of sophisticated equipment that lined the walls. In the middle of the room were two large screens on wheels and a white cannon hung from the ceiling – like the one Slapperton had used on William during the experiment.

William stood motionless for a few seconds, debating whether he should continue – but he had made it this far and he willed himself to keep going. As he came closer to the screens, he heard a noise over the bleeping of the computers. *Puff … puff … puff,* over and over, like a small steam engine. Slowly, he grabbed one of the screens and pulled it aside. Nothing could have prepared him for what he saw.

On the floor in front of him was an elderly man with grey hair and a beard. He was wearing a suit jacket, but everything below his waist was trapped inside a large square slab of steel – almost as if the metal had melted beneath him. The man was stuck inside the steel, like a bug encased in amber. William knew it was impossible – no one could survive being dipped into burning-hot molten steel.

The man's eyes were closed and he had an oxygen mask over his nose and mouth. A tube ran from his mask to a breathing machine that pumped air into his lungs. William stepped closer and stared at him with a mix of curiosity and dread. Was this the mysterious thing that the door had been talking about?

"Hello?" William said.

The man didn't react. William moved closer again and read the name tag: *Pontus Dippel. Depository for Impossible Archaeology.* The door had said that something had been moved from the Depository to a sonic laboratory in the basement. William studied the old man's wrinkled face, then leaned forward and touched his hand. It was warm. William looked up at the big white cannon that was pointing straight down at them. What were they planning on doing to this poor man?

The man's body suddenly jerked like he'd been jolted by electricity. His eyes flew open and he screamed at the top of his lungs, "SHE'S COMING ... SHE'S COMING!"

William backed away. He stood there staring in terror at the old man, who twisted and turned, trying to get free.

"SHE'S COMING..." the man shouted again.

"Please, calm down!" William shouted desperately.

Then the man's eyes closed and his head tilted forwards.

William heard an electric hum behind him. Three guard-bots rushed towards him and one raised its passivator. Before William had time to react, a beam shot out and hit him. His whole body went limp and he fell to the floor like a wet towel.

CHAPTER 11

Two guard-bots stopped in front of a white door. They were carrying William between them on a stretcher. His body was completely wobbly, as if all his bones had turned to jelly. William couldn't move a muscle – only his eyes – but his hands and feet had started to tingle and he hoped that meant the crazy jelly-technology was finally wearing off.

There was a soft hum as the door opened and the guard-bots continued into a room. They stopped in front of a large leather chair and helped William into it. He had just about enough control over his body now to stay upright. Large bookshelves loomed over him from all sides and he started to recognize the mahogany desk in front of him. He had been here before.

William could see a silhouette of a tall man with a cane standing by the window with his back to him. Finally, the man turned to face him.

"You don't waste much time, do you, William?"

William recognized the voice right away.

"How do you feel?" the man asked.

"A little shaky," William said, watching as Fritz Goffman approached him. Goffman was the head of the Institute, and one of the people who had saved William from Abraham Talley four months earlier. It was thanks to Goffman that Abraham hadn't succeeded in extracting all the luridium from William's body.

"It's completely normal to feel a little shaky after passivization," Goffman said and walked away.

William glanced up at Goffman's tall figure. His long arms hung down the sides of his skinny body, and the sun glistened off his black suit. Goffman pulled up his sleeve and glanced at the large watch that he wore on one of his sinewy wrists. The gesture seemed like a habit. Even with his back towards William, it was easy to tell that he wasn't pleased.

"The Institute owes you a debt of gratitude, William." Goffman cleared his throat. "But that doesn't mean you can walk around the building and go wherever you want – particularly not under these circumstances. The porter-bot you ditched was so distraught that it had lost you that it had a nervous breakdown, and was rushed down to Maintenance. It's traumatized. It's even talking about re-schooling."

William felt bad. He hadn't meant for the porter-bot to get into trouble.

"Are you thirsty?" Goffman asked, nodding at something behind William.

William slowly turned around and spotted two red-headed chauffeur-bots. These human-looking robots were Goffman's personal assistants. One of them walked over to a small table where there were glasses and drinks, and handed William a glass containing an orange liquid.

"Drink it," Goffman said. "It'll pick you up right away."

William eyed the orange beverage.

"Relax, it's Mars juice," Goffman said. "A new kind. It'll give you your strength back."

William took a swig of the Mars juice, which turned blue in a flash. It changed flavours while it was in his mouth – from orange to something like strawberry, and then vanilla. It tasted heavenly and he could feel a warm sensation spreading through his body. William sat up, moved his fingers and stretched his legs. He had full control of his body again. He made a mental note to stay away from passivators in the future.

"There was a man down there," William said, handing the glass back. "He was trapped in some kind of metal slab."

A serious expression came over Goffman's face. He cleared his throat again and tightened his grip on his cane, fumbling a little.

"A man … in a metal slab?" Goffman said. "Inside the room where the guard-bots found you?"

"Yes!" William said. "He was about my grandfather's age. It looked like the block had somehow melted around him."

William swallowed. He knew it sounded insane but, then again, surely Goffman knew about the man already.

"William…" began Goffman, leaning against the large desk, "I spoke with Benjamin Slapperton today about how your tests went…"

William sat up in the chair. "What does that have to do with this?" William asked.

"He said that you … saw something when he was testing you," Goffman said. "That you hallucinated."

"Yes…" William said. "But that had nothing to do with what I saw in that room. There really was a man, and he really was stuck…"

Goffman gave William a look, like he felt sorry for him. William sat back in the chair again.

"Would you like to know what I think?" Goffman asked. "I think that what you experienced in the basement was some kind of side effect from the experiment Benjamin performed on you in the lab."

"But, there was a man—"

"Listen to me, William … there is nothing down there. The guard-bots found you in one of the empty sonic laboratories," Goffman said. "They thought you were an intruder, and had no choice but to passivize you."

William could hardly believe what he was hearing. "So, you're… Are you saying that I was hallucinating?"

Goffman sat watching William for what felt like for ever.

"I suppose it's a disappointment to come back and find every-thing like this?" he finally said.

William looked at the floor. He felt really let down – he couldn't understand why Goffman didn't believe him.

"None of us are enjoying it either," Goffman continued. "The Institute hasn't been the same since Abraham was moved here – the thought of him lying down there in the basement has made people nervous. It's like he gives off some kind of negative energy … an energy that works even when he's in cold storage."

William looked up at him again. He felt a rush of frustra-tion surging through him. "What's wrong with me?" he asked, his voice trembling. "I want to know what's wrong with me."

Goffman nodded to the two chauffeurs, who turned and walked out of the room. Then he moved behind his enormous desk and sat down in his chair. Goffman rested his cane against the desk and took off his glasses. He cleaned them on the lapel of his jacket before putting them back on again.

"I want the same thing as you, William." Goffman clasped his hands and leaned towards him. "And that's why I have Benjamin running tests on you – to find out exactly what's causing your attacks. Meanwhile, you must take it easy until we find out."

"What about my grandfather?" William asked. "Why did he leave me here without even finding out what was wrong with me?"

"Tobias would have stayed if he could," Goffman said, his hands tightening until his knuckles turned white. "But there are very important matters that he had to take care of."

"Like the woman who attacked me outside my school?" William asked, frowning at Goffman.

"Yes, Tobias told me about that. I don't want you to worry," Goffman said, wandering over to the window. "You're safe here."

"But who is she and what did she want?" William asked. Nobody seemed to want to give him a straight answer.

"We're looking into it," Goffman said simply and turned towards William.

They sat in silence for a while. William studied Goffman's face for any sign of betrayal but, like all the members of the Institute, he was trained in keeping secrets – and he was very good at it.

"There's one other thing," Goffman said. "It's very important that you don't solve any more codes. Not before Benjamin has found the reason for your attacks."

William nodded. This was the second time since he'd arrived that someone had told him not to solve codes, and he didn't like it. As they sat there looking at each other, William knew that he had to find out more about the old man in the basement *and* the strange woman that had attacked him. He had a feeling that somehow these things would give him the answer to what was causing his attacks.

CHAPTER 12

When the meeting with Goffman was over, two porter-bots collected William. Their orders were to take him directly back to his room. William knew that Goffman wouldn't take any chances after his little excursion to the basement. As he slowly followed the robots down the hallway, he started to dread the thought of being cooped up in his room again – it really was starting to feel like a prison. William's feet were still a little wobbly after the passivization, and he was having a hard time keeping up with the porter-bots.

"Could we make a quick pit stop?" he asked.

"No," one of the porter-bots said. "We're heading directly to your room."

"There's someone I need to talk to." William had to get hold of Iscia. He knew that she would help him find out more about the old man in the secret room.

"Who?" the other porter-bot said.

"Iscia," William said. "She's one of the Field Agents – I know where her room is."

"Forget it," the porter-bot said. "We have orders."

For a split second, William considered giving the robots the slip, but then he thought better of it – he didn't want to risk getting passivized again.

"Here we are," one of the porter-bots said as they stopped outside William's room.

The door opened and William went inside. He turned and looked at the two porter-bots still standing in the hallway as the door slid shut.

"Welcome," the door said.

"Thanks." William said to the door. "I need to get hold of someone. Can you help me?"

"Haven't you been in enough trouble already?" the door asked.

"I can't even talk to any of my friends here at the Institute?" William said. "What is this, a prison?"

"I've got pastries on the way," the door said. "You hungry?"

"No, thank you," William said and took a step closer. "Can you help me or not?"

"Who is it that you want to talk to?" the door said.

"Iscia," William said.

"Iscia who?" the door asked.

"You know who." William was getting annoyed now.

"OK," the door said. "I'll see what I can do."

William walked over to the bed and lay down. He stared straight above like he had done so many times before, watching the light as it filtered through the trees outside and cast abstract shapes on the ceiling. The moving shapes relaxed him and his eyes started to feel heavy.

William jolted awake and sat up in bed, looking around the room. How long had he been asleep? His body was still sore, but he swung his legs over the side of the bed and got up. A sound made him look towards the door – the handle was moving … someone was trying to get in.

William froze.

"Door…?" he whispered. "Are you there?"

"Shh!" the door said. "There's someone out there. You have no scheduled visitors. Stand back."

William stepped away from the door. It was supposed to be burglar-proof, so he tried to reassure himself that there wasn't any danger. Then the door handle moved again.

"Can't you do something about this?" William asked.

The door didn't answer. William looked around for anything he could use to defend himself. His eyes stopped on the chair in front of his desk, but his heart sank as he remembered that it was bolted to the floor.

"They're opening the door using the code input panel," the door said.

"Can't you stop them?" William asked.

"They have forehead clearance and the code. There's not much I can do."

"So call a guard-bot!"

"I did. It'll be here in a couple of minutes," the door said. "We're on our own until then. Any ideas?"

"S–s–seriously?" William stammered.

Adrenaline shot through his body as he heard three quick beeps from the door. It opened with a *click*. William had no choice but to stand there, and wait. Nothing happened. Then a figure jumped into the doorway. William leaped backwards, crashed into the chair behind him and fell to the floor.

"Hahahahahahaha…!" someone laughed at him.

William recognized the laugh and looked up. Iscia was standing by the doorway giggling so hard that she could hardly stay upright. She looked different, more grown-up than the last time William had seen her, even though she was in fits of laughter.

"That wasn't funny, Iscia," he said, irritated, and got to his feet.

Back home in Norway, he had often thought about what he would say to her when he finally saw her again – what he'd just said was far from what he'd imagined. His face felt hot and he realized that he was blushing.

"You should have seen yourself. Your eyes were *soooo* big." She demonstrated with her fingers and chuckled.

They stood there looking at each other for a while. In the end, William couldn't help it any longer. A huge grin spread across his face. He was really pleased to see her again.

"When did you get back?" she asked.

"Earlier today," William said.

"Why didn't you let me know?"

"I tried," William said. "They told me you were busy."

"Busy?" Iscia said. "I'm not that busy."

"How did you find out I was here?"

"Your door contacted me through the intranet," she said, closing it behind her.

"Good," William said and looked at the door. He knew he could count on it.

"Always nice to have guests anyway," the door said. The hatch opened and a mechanical arm shot out, holding a steaming hot cupcake in front of Iscia's face.

"Thank you," Iscia said with a surprised smile and took the cupcake. The mechanical hand pulled back and the hatch in the door snapped shut. "You seem shaken," she said, taking a bite of the cake. "Did I frighten you that much?"

"I got passivized today," William said, scratching his arm.

"It usually itches for hours afterwards," Iscia said through a mouthful of cake.

"It doesn't itch, but it's kind of tingly…" William said, still rubbing his arm. "Have you had it done to you?"

"Yeah … that was part of our training when we went from being candidates to Field Agents," she said. "Being passivized definitely sucks."

77

William nodded in agreement. "How did you manage to get in here?"

"It goes with my job. I'm out in the field now – the clearance comes with that."

"So what are you doing now?" William asked. He was dying of curiosity to find out what she was up to.

"It's confidential," she said. "I can't say anything about it."

"I won't tell anyone," William said, disappointed. Was she going to start keeping secrets now, too?

"It's different now – I have to follow the rules."

William gave her a hard stare.

"OK, OK," she said and smiled. It was like she wanted him to drag it out of her. "I look after stuff…" she said and paused.

"Sounds boring." William sat on the bed.

"It's not." She came over and sat next to him, swivelling to face him. "It's old stuff – some of it's not even supposed to exist. There, I told you. Now it's your turn. Why have they done this to your room? And what happened to you on TV… Is everything OK?"

William hesitated. "I keep having these attacks," he said and looked away.

"Attacks?" she asked, leaning closer to him. "What kind of attacks?"

"They think it's because of the luridium. Apparently it's … uh … out of control – that's why they renovated my room," William said, avoiding eye contact. "I get these shooting headaches, like my head is about to explode … and then … I see things." He stopped and looked at her to check her reaction.

"You see things?" Iscia said. "What kind of things?"

"I don't know," William said. "Strange things – surreal stuff, like you might see in a nightmare. Have you ever had those dreams where you realize that you are dreaming?"

"Yes," Iscia said.

"It's like that," William said. "It feels completely real, but I'm not sure that it is. It's really creepy."

"Do you know what's causing it?" Iscia asked.

"Slapperton ran some tests on me. He's working on some kind of machine," William said. "He called it a particle frequency manipulator."

"A … what?" Iscia said.

"It's supposed to duplicate whatever triggers my attacks. It's got something to do with sound waves," William said and paused for a moment. "At least that's what he says."

"Don't you trust him?" she asked, peering at him.

"It's more like they don't trust me," William said. "Goffman says I'm hallucinating – because of the luridium – but I know what I saw."

"What are you talking about?" she asked, fidgeting.

"I saw something … down in the basement… You're going to think I'm crazy, too," he said.

"Right, except that I already know you're crazy." She laughed and punched him on the shoulder.

"I saw a man." William stood up. "He was stuck in the middle of a metal slab." Iscia looked at him. "It was as if the floor had melted and he had sunk into it like quicksand and then hardened again."

Iscia sat for a while, gazing into thin air. Her brown eyes intensified.

"You believe me, right?"

"I believe you," she said. "It's just … I'm really not meant to say anything."

"About what?" William demanded.

"There was an … incident."

"What happened?" William said, remembering what the robot had said about the raising of the security level.

"It's unclear." Iscia got up. "But, there's someone here at the Institute who shouldn't be here … an intruder."

"Someone's hiding at the Institute?" William said. "Who?"

"They don't know. They picked up a blurry figure on the surveillance cameras. It comes and goes through walls…" she whispered. "I don't know any more about it, but it's freaking everyone out."

William stood there, lost in thought. *An intruder, here at the Institute?* Then his heart started to beat faster. He had met someone who could seemingly evaporate at will. The woman from outside his school. Was it possible that she was the mysterious figure who had broken into the Institute?

"Come on. I have to show you what I saw – you're the only

one who believes me," William said and turned to the door. "Door, we need to get out."

"Not again…" the door said.

"Yes … again," William demanded.

"They won't send a porter-bot this late."

"Good," William said and looked at Iscia. "We won't be needing one. She's a Field Agent."

CHAPTER 13

William and Iscia stood in the lift. It hummed as they moved downwards and gentle music played from a small speaker in the ceiling.

"Level 1A," the lift said.

"I'm sure we're going to get in *big* trouble for this," Iscia said as the doors opened with a *ding*.

"And *I'm* sure this is something you'll want to see," William replied, walking out. "Besides … when did getting in a little bit of trouble worry you so much?"

"When they gave me more responsibility," Iscia said, following him.

William sped up. He wanted to get into the laboratory where the old man was before they were discovered. He had to see it with his own eyes again and show Iscia so that she could help him.

"It's so creepy that someone's sneaking around the Institute and no one knows who it is," Iscia said. She shuddered as they moved down the dark hallway.

"Iscia listen, it's going to sound weird, but I think I might know who it is," William said. He had planned on finding out more about the woman who had attacked him outside his school before telling Iscia, but he didn't want to hide it from her – especially if the woman was responsible for the problems at the Institute.

"Her?" Iscia said, stopping in her tracks.

"The one they're afraid of," William said. "At least, I think it must be her."

"Where did you see her?" Iscia asked and grabbed his arm. "At the Institute?"

"No … she attacked me outside my school in Norway," William said. "She wanted me to go with her."

"Wait, someone tried to kidnap you in Norway? Why didn't you tell me?" Iscia said.

"My grandfather said that it was nothing … that I would be safe here. But the woman I saw… I think that she could somehow disappear at will. And if that's true, perhaps she can walk through walls too."

"And you've seen her, here at the Institute?" Iscia asked.

"Well, no…"

"Then we can't know it's her for sure… What did she look like?"

"I'll tell you more when we're not in such a hurry. I need

to go back to the laboratory first – I need to make sure that what I saw was real." William continued down the hallway and turned the corner at the end of it. "OK. Here we are. Can you use your clearance to open the door?"

Iscia stopped next to him. "I know I'm going to regret this," she whispered.

William looked at her. He could see the glint in her eyes, indicating that part of her was enjoying this adventure. Iscia walked over to the control panel, leaned in and put her forehead to the scanner. A laser-beam travelled across and back over her forehead.

"Disapproved," the computer voice said flatly.

Iscia pulled away from the wall. She looked at it, startled.

"That's strange," she said. "I have universal clearance."

She leaned in and tried again, but the computer rang out with the same reply.

"What's going on?" Iscia said, looking baffled.

"They must have changed the codes," William said. He knew only he could break the code and that would mean disobeying Goffman's orders. But William had to know if he could trust his own senses – he had to know if what he saw was real. He made a decision. "Let me try."

Iscia moved to the side. William walked over to the control panel and focused his attention on it. He could feel the vibrations starting at the bottom of his spine. He closed his eyes and let the vibrations travel up his spine and out into his arms and fingers. He had never got completely used to this feeling – it was like there was something controlling his body – and since he'd started having the attacks, the sensation of the luridium moving inside him felt more alien than ever.

William opened his eyes and looked at the control panel. The digits had lit up and slowly started swapping places. The *nine* travelled upwards on the panel and swapped places with the *three*, like one of those mechanical puzzle games where little squares are moved around to make an image. Then the digits started mixing together, multiplying and forming long rows of flowing numbers in front of him. His fingers flew across the panel, hovering after the moving digits.

William pressed the buttons on the control panel one after the other – faster and faster. Soon he realized that whoever had been fiddling with the control panel since he was last here hadn't changed the code – they had completely deleted it. But there was still a universal code that would probably unlock all of the doors at the Institute.

William pressed the final button, and the light disappeared from the digits. The vibrations subsided and he was back in reality. He looked at Iscia, then at the control panel. Had he cracked the code?

"Approved," a flat voice said from inside the little speaker on the control panel. William shot Iscia a quick look and smiled. She didn't look pleased.

"Oh, you're such a genius," she said.

"It's not your fault." William pushed on the door. "They clearly don't want anyone to go in here."

"So maybe we shouldn't," she said and peeked into the lab.

"Come on," William could tell that she was still curious about what was inside. "But keep a lookout for guard-bots."

They continued into the room and the door closed behind them with a *click*.

"Wow … it looks like a space station," her eyes took in the gigantic room. She was clearly impressed. "And what's that over there?" Iscia said, pointing to the large cannon and the two floating screens in the middle of the room.

"That's where he is," William said.

"I don't know if this is such a good idea." It seemed like she was having second thoughts.

"I want to hear you say that you can see him, too. I need to have someone to back me up." He pulled her along. They stopped in front of the large screens that looked like floating walls. "Are you ready?" he whispered.

She nodded.

"I should warn you, it's a disturbing sight." William paused for a few seconds then pulled one of the screens aside.

Iscia burst out laughing.

"Is it not possible to get any privacy around here?" a voice said.

William stood there and stared. The main in the slab of steel had gone. Instead, there was a robot sitting in a deckchair

86

reading a newspaper. William remembered the argu-bot from the first time he came to the Institute. It was one of the first robots he had met when he had arrived – especially designed to be difficult and create arguments.

"What are you doing here?" William asked.

"I could ask the same of you," the argu-bot said. "And not that it's any of your business, but I'm trying to enjoy some hard-earned down time."

"Where did the old man go?" William demanded, moving closer.

"What old man?" the argu-bot asked, leaning back in his chair.

"The old man who was here," William said, his voice trembling. "He was stuck in a huge piece of metal." William turned to Iscia. "This is *not* what I saw – there was an old man."

"I'm not old, and I'm far from retirement," the argu-bot said, testily.

William ignored the robot. "They must have moved him." He scanned the floor.

"We should go," Iscia said.

Suddenly, William spotted a little piece of white plastic on the floor, right under the deckchair where the robot was sitting. It looked like a name tag. William moved towards the chair.

"What are you doing?" the argu-bot said.

"I need to have a look at something under your chair," William said.

"You need to stop invading my personal space," the argu-bot replied. "I'm a very private robot."

"A quick look," William said.

"That's exactly what my ex-wife used to say," the argu-bot said. "And look where that got me. She ran off with the gardener-bot."

William had had enough – he needed to get his hands on that name tag. "OK, then," William said and started to turn, but with a quick movement, he pretended to stumble and fell towards the deckchair. He landed on top of the startled argu-bot and rolled to the floor.

"What are you doing?" the argu-bot yelled. "You need to respect my space."

"I'm sorry," William said as he got to his feet and pocketed the name tag. He turned to Iscia. "Let's get out of here."

CHAPTER 14

"William, wait!" Iscia said, jogging after him as he strode down the hallway. "A name tag doesn't prove anything."

"So now *you* don't believe me?" William said, continuing up the stairs. He looked down at the name tag that read: *Pontus Dippel: Depository for Impossible Archaeology.*

"I—" Iscia began, taking the stairs two at a time to catch up with him.

"Do you know who Pontus Dippel is?" William asked.

Iscia hesitated long enough for William to know that she was holding back on something.

"Do you?" he demanded.

She shook her head and looked down. That only made William angrier. He turned and continued up the stairs.

"They were keeping him captive. I know it," he said. "They experimented on him and then they must have moved him somewhere else after I discovered him."

"That's not how the Institute works," Iscia said.

"What, like you know everything there is to know about the Institute?" William asked as he reached the top of the stairs.

"I know quite a bit, actually," she said.

"But not everything," William said before stopping again. He turned to face her and waved the name tag in front of her. "This is enough proof for me that he was there. They're holding him captive somewhere in the Institute and I'm going to find out—"

"Find out what?" a voice said from behind him.

William turned around and saw Freddy standing a little way away. William stuffed the name tag in his pocket. Freddy had given William a hard time when he first came to the Institute and, after William had crushed his orb in an orb duel, William was sure Freddy wouldn't go any easier on him this time around.

"You're not allowed to move around this place without a porter-bot," Freddy said.

"He's with me," Iscia said.

William stared at Freddy's freckled face. He wasn't planning on being pushed around by him, but Freddy had grown quite a bit since the last time he'd seen him; he was now almost a full head taller than William.

"What were you guys doing down there?" he asked, nodding towards the stairs.

"We took a wrong turn," William said.

"I would say so," Freddy said with a glance at Iscia.

"Come on," Iscia said, pulling William along, but Freddy moved in front of them and blocked their way.

"I haven't seen you in a while, William. Where have you been?" Freddy asked, scrutinizing William again with his beady eyes. "I haven't forgotten what you did to my orb."

"Leave him alone, Freddy," Iscia said.

William had known that one day he would have to deal with Freddy; only now, he didn't have an orb to help defend him.

"I just want to say," Freddy whispered and leaned closer, "that I've forgiven you."

William was caught completely off guard. This was the last thing he'd expected to hear from Freddy, the Institute's biggest bully.

"You're kidding, right?"

"I'm not kidding," Freddy said and gave William a fatherly pat on the shoulder. "Orb duels are for children. We're beyond that now, and some of us have become Field Agents." Freddy glanced over at Iscia with a knowing smile.

William didn't get what was going on. Was Freddy a Field Agent now – for the Institute?

"Come on. Let's go," Iscia said and pulled William along by his arm.

"Wait," Freddy said, glancing at Iscia. "You haven't told him … have you?"

"I–I—" Iscia's eyes widened.

William looked at her. *Told him what?*

"Iscia and I—" Freddy began and then paused—"are a team now."

A cold shiver ran through William's body. A *team*? He gave Iscia a bewildered look.

"We work together," Iscia quickly added. "The Institute teamed us up… I was planning on telling you. But you were so preoccupied with … with the, well, you know … that I didn't have a chance to say anything—"

"No unapproved loitering in the hallways!" a flat computer voice interrupted Iscia as a guard-bot came rolling towards them, pointing its passivator at them.

"Whoops, I've got to get going," Freddy said with a big grin. "Great to see you again, William. Are you coming, Iscia?"

Freddy nodded and Iscia turned to William. "William … I—" She didn't have a chance to say any more before the guard-bot interrupted her again.

"I repeat: you cannot loiter here. Move along!" the guard-bot said to them. Then he turned to William, "You, come with me."

Freddy and Iscia headed down the hallway with the porter-bot. Iscia glanced back at William before they vanished around a corner.

CHAPTER 15

William turned to the robot standing in the doorway of his room. A little red lamp on the side of the porter-bot's head flashed – a transmission was taking place.

"Benjamin Slapperton is looking for you," the porter-bot said. "He's already on his way here."

William hadn't slept a wink all night. He sat on the floor, leaned his head against the wall and closed his eyes for a moment. What had happened to the woman with the mechanical hand? Why was no one telling him the truth about the old man? And how could Iscia be working with Freddy? So many things at the Institute had changed, and William was now even more sceptical about the experiment Slapperton was performing on him. Did he know what he was doing, and could William trust him?

William looked up as the sound of Benjamin's hover-cart came closer to the open door. The cart was travelling at great speed, and it slammed into the wall when it stopped.

"I don't want to be out here in the hallways any longer than necessary," Benjamin shouted over the noise from the fan. "You need to hurry, something terrible has happened – get in, quickly!"

"What's wrong?" William asked as he got to his feet and jumped in next to Benjamin.

"The cockroach vanished during the night. "There's no sign of a break-in and nothing on the security cameras. This is an absolute catastrophe – we have an out-of-control cockroach filled with luridium running loose around the Institute!" Benjamin shot William a nervous look. "There's no time to lose. William, I'm afraid I'm going to have to ask you to go through more experiments. We have to find the source of the sound waves and we have to hurry."

A few minutes later, Benjamin was busy strapping William into the chair. William looked up at the white cannon above him.

"There was a cannon like this pointing at the old man that I saw in the basement," William said and turned to Benjamin. "He was stuck in some kind of metal slab."

Benjamin, who was fiddling with some wires inside the control box, stopped what he was doing. "I don't know any-thing about that." It sounded rehearsed.

"And then, when I went back there, the old man was gone," William said, goading Benjamin to tell him the truth.

"You shouldn't roam around the Institute on your own," Benjamin said and closed the panel on the side of the box. "What if you had an attack?"

He got to his feet and gave William a serious look. "It's dangerous, William. You know that." Benjamin pointed at the chair. "Since the last time, I've added some more straps on each armrest and one for your waist – it's for your own safety. Do you mind?"

William gulped. He didn't like the thought of being strapped into the chair.

"OK…" he said.

Benjamin quickly strapped William's hands to the armrests and fastened a belt around his waist. He gave William a quick pat on the shoulder. "Are you ready?" he asked.

William nodded. Benjamin passed him a little black box with a red button on it.

"For the sake of the experiment, I need you to bear it for as long as you can. But if it becomes too much for you, press the button and the cannon will turn off. OK?"

"OK," William said, tensing his fingers around the little box. He leaned back in the chair and closed his eyes. He felt Benjamin put ear defenders on him and everything went quiet. The particle frequency manipulator above him started humming. At first, the noise was so faint that he could hardly hear it. Then it started to become louder and William could feel the sound waves travelling through his body.

The rumbling at the base of his spine began. Then the cold spread up his back and out into his arms. William tightened his grip on the black box. He didn't want to press it ... not yet. He wanted to see what would happen next. The cold continued to his hands and then the headache struck. It was as if someone had hit him in the forehead. He shut his eyes and gritted his teeth together, trying not to scream. Even though his hands were shaking, he had to fight to keep from pressing the red button.

Must not press ... must not press...

The rumbling disappeared, and everything went quiet. When William opened his eyes, he was standing in the big cavernous hall with the high stone walls. As before, a large golden ring hovered above him and he could see the same white coffin on wheels standing on the ground below. There was something menacing about the oblong box. Once again, William felt like he should somehow know what it was...

He started to walk towards the white container, but pulled back as the lid of the box opened. A frosty mist seeped out and weaved its way down towards the floor like a snake. A hand appeared from inside the box. William wanted to turn away – close his eyes – but he couldn't. He just stood there, staring at the hand.

"WILLIAM?" someone shouted from the darkness.

William blinked. He was back in the lab.

"WILLIAM?" he heard again – his ear defenders made it

96

hard to hear where the sound was coming from. He looked around and saw Benjamin floating in the air in front of him, a few metres above the floor. He was flailing his arms around like crazy and pointing at William.

"PUSH THE BUTTON!"

William looked down at the little remote control he was still holding in his shaking hand. He slowly pushed down the button with his thumb and the sound cannon stopped humming. The cold in his body disappeared and he watched as Benjamin crashed to the floor.

"I know what's causing it," Benjamin said, unsteadily getting to his feet and hurrying over to his desk. "I know what's causing it…"

"What?" William asked, struggling to get out of the chair – momentarily forgetting that he had been strapped in.

Benjamin searched through the clutter and found a small notepad and a pencil. He wrote something on the pad, tore the page off and stuffed it in his pocket.

"What did you find out?" William shouted.

"Oh, sorry," Benjamin said. He removed the straps around William and helped him out of the chair. "I have to do some more calculations – but I'll tell you as soon as I've figured it out."

"But you said you knew what it was?" William said, rubbing his wrists.

"Yes … I found a sub-frequency of sound waves that causes

levitation." He paused. "There's only one source I know of that produces waves like that. But if it's what I think it is … it can't be possible."

"It's impossible?" William said.

"Yes," Benjamin said. "Impossible."

CHAPTER 16

William sat on his bed, staring into space. He kept thinking about the mysterious floating ring and the figure in the box. What did it all mean? And what was the impossible thing that Benjamin had discovered? He walked over to the window and looked through the bars and the hanging vines that curled over the glass. Only a few months ago – on his first visit to the Institute – he had found this view the most amazing in the world. But now vehicles were patrolling the white wall that fenced in the vast park and a surveillance drone whizzed past his window.

As he stood there, lost in his own thoughts, he heard something in the room – a faint tapping somewhere behind him. William turned around. The tapping was gone. Then it started again – this time louder. William took a step forward, but froze as a cockroach shot across the floor in front of him and scurried towards a dark corner on the other side of the room.

And that's when William saw it – someone standing in the corner, completely still. The cockroach stopped and the figure bent down and positioned its mechanical hand so that the cockroach could climb onto it. Then the person straightened up again and looked at William. It was as if time had stopped. He could smell burnt rubber – like the air in the room had become toxic – and felt like he couldn't breathe. William turned and groped around for something to defend himself with, but his hand found only air. He backed up and hit the wall by the window. He wanted to shout out for help but just stood there, completely paralyzed.

The figure took a step towards him and into the light. William gasped. It was the same woman who had attacked him outside his school. She was wearing dark sunglasses, her unkempt hair covered half her face and a long, black coat came all the way down to her knees. Her mechanical hand was covered in strange symbols that William had never seen before.

"It hurts doesn't it?" the woman said in a raspy voice.

"What hurts?" The words seemed to fall out of William's mouth.

"Not belonging," the woman said. "Being in the middle."

She removed her dark sunglasses. Her eyes looked completely wild. One of them darted back and forth as if it were following an invisible fly. Then the light fell on the other side of her face. The skin was red and had started to curl, as if it had been badly burnt.

"You're a freak, William. Like me. You're neither human or machine. You're in the middle too. You're basically … nothing."

William tried to keep from panicking completely, but adrenaline surged through his body, making it impossible to think clearly. He was out-powered and knew he didn't stand a chance against this woman. He tried to call out to the door, but the woman held up her hand.

"I wouldn't bother if I were you … it can't hear you." She looked at the insect running up her arm. "I thought I had lost it for good … then I stumbled across it here, in one of the laboratories. Isn't that crazy?"

William stood there, unable to answer.

"This little thing has enough luridium in it to tip the scale. All it takes is for you to touch it, and the luridium would leave its little body and enter yours. Then you would be more machine than human. That would be much better for you. Then you would at least be … something."

William looked at the insect. For a split second, he wondered what it would be like to touch it. The woman had a hypnotic effect on him – it was as though her voice came from inside his head, almost as if she could speak directly to his brain.

"A shame you won't get to it though. I would never let you hurt it. We've been friends for a long time."

"How did you get in here?" William asked, casting a quick glance at the closed door.

"I have my ways," she said and grinned.

"What do you want?" William said, trying to hide the tremble in his voice.

"Like I said outside your stupid school, I need you to do something for me." The woman paused and stared at him with her wild eyes. "They haven't told you about what happened, have they?" Her grin exposed two rows of yellow teeth. "Keeping it all secret." She gestured with her arms.

"*What* happened?" William asked, but he already knew the answer.

"You've already seen it," she said.

"The man trapped in the metal?" William asked.

The woman didn't respond; she just stood there watching him with a smirk on her lips. William studied her, hoping that Goffman had been right – that he might find a sign that she was a hallucination – a product of his own brain playing a trick on him.

"You're going to do something for me," she said, her eyes narrowing.

William's heart beat so hard now that it felt like it would jump right out of his chest.

"If you help me," she said, "I will make your attacks go away."

"What is it you want me to do?" he asked.

"KNOCK, KNOCK," the door suddenly said.

The woman turned and hissed. "I'll see you again soon, William Wenton," she whispered and pushed one of the buttons on the mechanical hand, which started to emit a high-pitched sound. "If you tell anyone about me … I won't be so nice next time we meet. I might even take it out on your little girlfriend."

"Leave Iscia alone—" William shouted.

But the woman was gone in a *zap* and a flash of blue light. There was only smoke and a sickening smell of burnt rubber in the air.

"KNOCK, KNOCK," the door repeated before opening.

Iscia stood outside. "I feel so bad," she said and smiled apologetically.

William blinked, trying to compose himself. "Why?" he said shakily.

"Because of what happened yesterday – me not telling you about Freddy … not telling you about other things too…"

"That's OK," William said quickly.

"Are you all right?" Iscia said and looked at him. "Is something … burning?" She sniffed the air.

"Everything's great," William said, stepping out into the hallway and closing the door behind him.

"You sure?" she said. "You look like you've seen a ghost."

William nodded, unsure of what to say.

"OK… Well, I also came by because I wanted to make it up to you. There's something you should see," Iscia said. "It's to do with Pontus Dippel."

She gave him a quick nod, and the two of them started walking.

CHAPTER 17

William and Iscia were jogging through the park behind the Institute. The sun was setting and the tall trees cast long, dark shadows across the grass. Iscia dodged behind bushes and around trees with rehearsed movements, while William followed close behind her. They had managed to sneak past several guard-bots – but now they had a different problem: the security vehicles in the park.

William was still shaken from seeing the woman with the mechanical hand in his room. Whatever she wanted from him, he knew he'd have to find a way to protect himself – to protect Iscia. He couldn't tell her about the woman's visit, not without putting Iscia in danger too. He needed to find out what he was up against first and then work out what to do.

"I don't want you to think I'm hiding things from you," Iscia started, "so I want to show you what we've been up to."

"'We… as in you and Freddy?" William asked.

"I didn't have any choice – the Institute assigned us to work together," Iscia said. "Freddy's not so bad once you get to know him. It was his idea to take you here, you know."

"It was?" William asked.

Suddenly, she stopped and pulled William down behind a large shrub, then put her finger on her lips. They stayed still and waited for a few moments, then a small tank with a passivator on its roof stopped right in front of the bush. William could make out a camera mounted next to the little cannon as it swept over the area before driving off again. It didn't appear to have seen them.

"They have motion detectors," Iscia whispered, "but if we hold completely still, they should have a hard time detecting us."

"Where are we going?" William said.

"There," she said, pointing to the man-made pond in the middle of the park. Iscia checked to see if the coast was clear and got to her feet. "Come on."

William darted after her and soon they were running along the water's edge. It was a relief to be out in the fresh air, after spending so much time inside the Institute. It also felt good being with Iscia again.

The surface of the water was covered with white lilies. A little way out in the pond was a statue of a woman holding an orb over her head, which gave off a golden light. A couple of swans paddled past the statue. William was struck by how beautiful they looked compared to the rest of the park, which now resembled an exercise yard in a prison.

"Hurry up," Iscia whispered. "The swans get suspicious pretty quickly."

A swan turned around and looked at William with glowing red eyes.

"What, you're afraid of swans now?" William teased her with a grin.

"Those aren't normal swans," Iscia said.

William gazed at the white birds. One of the swans approached them, fluffing its feathers, then a little cannon popped up from a hatch on its back.

"They're cyborg swans!" William said, startled.

"Of course," Iscia said, tugging at him. "If we stand here for very long, they'll shoot. We have to get in there—" she pointed to a stone building by the edge of the water a little further away—"before they realize that you're not Freddy."

Two robots with passivators stood in front of the building.

"Guard-bots?" William said.

"I know," Iscia said. "They've been there since it happened."

"Since what happened?" William asked.

"Come." She scurried towards the building.

William cast a glance back over his shoulder. Both swans were staring at them now and had their cannons pointed in their direction. One of the big birds had already reached the shore and was stepping out of the water.

Iscia stopped in front of a solid-looking brass door, covered with scratches and oxidation marks. There was a round dial in the middle, like the lock on a safe.

"Halt!" one of the guard-bots suddenly called out and raised the passivator it was clutching in its metal hands.

"We have clearance," Iscia said.

The other guard-bot scanned her forehead. The light on the scanner changed colour from red to green.

"What about him?" the guard-bot said and pointed at William.

"He's with me," Iscia said.

"You may pass," the robot said and rolled to the side.

William stepped closer and ran his fingers over the rough surface of the door. He felt the rumbling begin in his stomach – the way it did whenever he started to think about a difficult code.

"It's old," he said, fascinated.

"Yes," Iscia said, "very old. It took me more than two weeks to crack it. It was one of the entrance requirements." Iscia looked over at the two swans that were waddling towards them. "We'd better hurry. The swans are smarter than the guard-bots," she whispered and turned the dial – first one way then the other – until the door made a faint *click* and slid open on its rusty hinges.

"Come on," she said, disappearing into the darkness within.

William cast one last glimpse back at the swans before ducking inside and pulling the door shut behind him.

CHAPTER 18

William and Iscia were standing in a large room with glass walls and a vaulted glass ceiling. It looked like an upside-down aquarium and William realized that the stairs had lead them underneath the pond where they'd just seen the swans swimming. Faint sunlight glimmered through the murky water above them and something that looked like a mechanical shark swam past the window.

"The dome's made of shatter-resistant glass," Iscia said. "This room belongs to part of the Institute that was built more than a hundred years ago. It's where the Institute keeps some of the most secret objects."

William stared into the darkness. The whole floor seemed to be made of steel but, here and there, patches of rust had formed from the occasional leak from the glass dome above.

"So this is the Depository?"

"Yes," Iscia said. "Or, to be more precise: the Depository for

Ancient Items No One Can Explain – well, that's my unofficial definition anyway."

She pressed a switch on the wall and an old brass light fixture in the ceiling flickered to life. William gasped as the room lit up, revealing hundreds of objects that were sealed in glass cases of all shapes and sizes. At first glance, the items looked like any old things you might find in a history museum. But as William began to examine the cases more closely, he could see that the objects within were anything but ordinary. His eyes rested on something sitting alone in a small case and he stopped short.

"Is that what I think it is?" he asked, so excited his voice was shaky.

"That depends on what you think it is," Iscia said.

"The London Hammer…" he whispered, looking at the item more closely.

"Correct."

Inside the case was a rusty old hammer with a wooden handle. It could have easily been mistkaen for a hammer that had been left in the rain for decades – but William had read about the object in one of his grandfather's books back home in Norway. The London Hammer had been found by an elderly couple out for a walk in a place called London, Texas. They had spotted a wooden handle sticking out of a rock and thought that was odd, so they took the rock to a laboratory. The scientists opened the rock and found an entire hammer perfectly preserved inside.

"How old is it?" William asked without taking his eyes off the hammer.

"Millions of years old." she said. "The hammer was trapped inside the dirt for so long that the dirt itself hardened and became rock. That's a process that takes millions of years."

"But that's long before there were people," William said. "Which means that in principle … it should be impossible for the hammer to exist."

"That's why it's here," Iscia said. "Everything in here is somehow impossible in one way or another – at least, based on what we know about the history of humans on Earth."

William had to force himself away from the hammer and continue among the display cases. He stopped in front of an enormous horizontal case in the middle of the room.

He gasped. "Now that can't be real!"

"It is," Iscia said.

There was a gigantic human skeleton lying in the case in front of them. William walked over to the skull and studied it through the glass – the skull alone was as tall as he was. He looked down the length of the enormous body and saw that the arms were stretched out along its sides. He'd seen pictures online of gigantic skeletons like this, but most of them had later been revealed to be fake.

"How old is it?" he asked.

"The tests that were run indicated an approximate age of

around four hundred million years," she said.

William noticed a wide crack in the skull's forehead.

"What's that?" he asked, pointing.

"The cause of death, I assume," she said. "They must have fallen or been hit on the head by something heavy. This skeleton was donated to us from an anonymous private collector in Egypt. He didn't dare hold on to it any longer. Impossible archaeology is a very dangerous business, you know."

"Why?" William asked.

Iscia hesitated. "Because there are a lot of people out there who don't want the truth to come out," she finally said.

William looked at her. "What truth?"

"The truth about our whole history as a species on this planet," Iscia said.

"What do you mean?" William said, looking at her with a steady gaze.

"Well, for a start, we have been on earth much longer than most people think," Iscia said slowly.

"And how long is that?" William asked.

"Look around," she said and pointed at all the artefacts that surrounded them. "Many of these man-made objects are millions of years old."

"So?" William said. "Why does it matter how long we've been here?"

"It matters to a lot of people," Iscia said. "Can you imagine the ramifications if it came out that humans had been on Earth millions, instead of hundreds of thousands of years? Our whole history would have to be rewritten."

"I get it," William said. "People aren't ready for the truth."

"Something like that," she said. "So we keep it stored and catalogued here, until one day it becomes … public."

"When the public is ready?" William added.

Iscia nodded. William thought it was strange that part of mankind's history had to be hidden away – that it could even be considered dangerous. Why was it that people found anything out of the ordinary so threatening? But then William thought about the luridium inside of him. He remembered how his teacher back home in Norway had treated him. William knew it was because Mr Humburger was afraid of him – because William was different, and in certain ways, a lot smarter than him. Maybe people weren't ready for him either.

William looked at the giant skeleton again. "He must have been more than thirty metres tall," he said, pointing at it.

"She," Iscia said. "She was female."

"Wow," William said. "Do you think there were giants on earth?"

"After I started working here, I realized one thing," Iscia said and paused.

"What was that?" William said.

"That most things are possible," she said, her gaze wandering around the overcrowded room. "I thought you'd like seeing this," she continued and moved further into the space. "What do you think about that over there?" she asked, pointing to something on the far wall.

William's mouth dropped open when he saw a glass cabinet with a stone robot inside it. He stopped in front of it – instantly recognizing his grandfather's swooping handwriting as he read the label: *3.8-million-year-old exoskeleton.*

"That's one of the oldest exoskeletons we've found," Iscia said.

"Three point eight million years old?" William mumbled in disbelief. "Who could have made it?"

"We're not sure," Iscia said.

"How was it powered?" William asked. "Electricity?"

"We have no idea," Iscia said and scratched her head. "And neither does Benjamin or anyone else here at the Institute. They collect all this stuff from around the world and then bring it here for further examination, then we try to replicate the most interesting ancient technology. We've actually done lots of work on creating exoskeletons like this one."

"I know," William said. "The Institute sent one for my father to try. It's really cool."

William was beginning to understand why there were so many people who wanted to keep these discoveries under wraps. If even one of the items in this room was authentic, it would rewrite world history.

"I'm sorry I didn't tell you," Iscia said.

He turned around and looked at her. "You mean about the man I saw in the room?" William said.

She nodded.

"You're not crazy," she said. "He's for real… Pontus Dippel was the curator for all of this," she said. "And something terrible did happen to him."

William remembered what it had said on the name tag he had found in the secret room: *Depository for Impossible Archaeology*.

"Come over here," she said, motioning to him. "There's more I want to show you."

CHAPTER 19

"That's where they found him," Iscia said and pointed to a large square hole in the floor in front of them.

"So, what happened to him?" William asked.

"Someone shot him with some kind of ray," Iscia said. "It was meant to kill him, but he survived – although he was left fused into the metal floor. They had to cut out a block and move him to a laboratory, where they're still trying to free him."

"Why didn't you tell me this before?" William asked.

"It's supposed to be top secret," she said. "I'm telling you now though – that must count for something?"

William nodded, feeling guilty that he hadn't told Iscia about the woman with the mechanical hand. Could she be responsible for this? He walked over to the edge and looked into the hole.

"Do you know who did it?" he asked.

Iscia was about to answer when William turned and saw

Freddy coming towards them. Iscia moved to stand beside William.

"Exciting, isn't it? All these fantastic objects." Freddy threw out his arms like a king showing someone his kingdom. "It doesn't surprise me that you're here. You must find this place really interesting."

William didn't say anything. He still didn't understand why Freddy was acting so friendly. It was a big change of character since the last time William had been at the Institute.

Freddy looked at Iscia. "So, have you shown him the orb yet?"

"What orb?" She looked puzzled.

"Didn't you know?" Freddy walked in between two large shelves. "Come on, William loves orbs – I'll show him!"

William looked at Iscia.

"We should leave," she said.

William felt a faint tingling in his stomach. It grew in strength and the vibrations started travelling up his spine. It was like an invisible force was pulling him forward, and he had no other choice than to start walking. Was he having another attack? He tried not to panic.

"Where are you going?" he heard Iscia say from behind him.

"I don't know," he said. "Something's happening."

He followed the direction that Freddy had gone in, and stopped when he got to the other end of the room. It was darker here. In front of him were even more rows of old glass cabinets, but some of them were covered with dusty cotton tarpaulins.

"This is the old stuff," Iscia said.

"I thought everything down here was old?" William said, trying to control the vibrations in the pit of his stomach.

"This stuff is so old it's undatable," she said. "I don't even know what's down here."

William continued. His eyes had adapted to the gloom and he spotted Freddy standing by an old cabinet – it was twice William's height, about two metres wide and partially covered with a grey tarpaulin. Freddy raised his hand, grabbed hold of the sheet and pulled it off.

"Freddy, I really don't think you should…" Iscia started.

Whatever was inside the cabinet was having a strong effect on William. He felt a force pulling him closer. It had to be some kind of code. William could make out the contours of a round object, about the size of a basketball. He took a step closer and leaned in until his forehead stopped at the glass. His eyes were locked on the object.

It was an orb made from brass, marked with deep dents and cuts and covered in strange symbols. William could feel the vibrations all over now. He wanted to hold the orb in his hands more than anything.

"That thing has to be really rare," he mumbled.

"It is," Freddy said. "Priceless…"

"So leave it alone," Iscia said. "If we broke it, we would be in big trouble."

117

William tried to fight the urge to open the cabinet door and lift the orb out. What would be the harm in holding it? He desperately wanted to, but he made himself take a couple of steps back. The vibrations subsided a little.

"Should we take it out for a closer look?" Freddy said. "I've always wondered what this orb could do."

"No," Iscia said firmly. "What's wrong with you two? We should leave."

"Why?" Freddy said. "It won't hurt to have a little fun – everything has become so serious around here. You're a genius, William. Don't you want to see if you can solve a puzzle that no one has ever solved before?"

"I'd better not," William said.

"You're just being modest." Freddy flicked up the latch on the glass door. Iscia went to stop him, but he ignored her and reached in for the orb and carefully lifted it out, holding it in both hands. "This is the real deal," he said. "Not like the fake ones they give us here at the Institute." He stared at it for a moment. "Do you know why they confiscated all of the real orbs?"

William shook his head. "Why?"

"Because orbs are powerful things – but you already know that, don't you, William?"

"Cut it out, Freddy," Iscia said, irritated. She tried to take the orb from him, but Freddy pulled it away.

"What do you say, William?" Freddy said, stepping closer

to him. "Don't you want to try it? It's bound to be too old to work anyway."

"Don't listen to him, William," Iscia said, pulling him by the arm.

But William was transfixed. It was as if the old orb was drawing his hands up. He could already feel the vibrations starting in his stomach again. As much as he tried to fight it, deep down William wanted to prove his ability to himself – after everything that had happened in the past couple of days, he needed to. Before he knew it, he had taken the orb from Freddy's hands – the vibrations spreading up his spine and into his arms the instant he touched it.

"William?" he heard Iscia say.

But it was too late now. Her voice sounded like it was coming from far away and William could only focus on the orb in front of him. His fingers set to work. The various parts were difficult to move at first – it had obviously been a long time since the orb had been used – but, little by little, as he twisted and turned them, the parts began to move. *Click … click … click.* Faster and faster.

William turned his head and caught sight of Freddy – grinning at him – and Iscia, watching on with concern. William knew in that instant that he'd made the wrong decision. He had no idea what this orb could do and he'd already been warned, several times, that solving codes could trigger an attack. How could he have let himself be talked into something that had the potential to be so dangerous?

He looked down at his fingers, which were flying over the orb – desperately focusing all of his energy on making them cut it out. But they wouldn't obey him. William tried harder, until his entire body was shaking uncontrollably with the effort. He pulled one hand back with all his might and the orb crashed to the floor.

William stood there staring at the orb, which lay motionless in front of him.

"If it's ruined, it's your fault," Freddy snapped.

"You're the one who egged him on, you fool," Iscia said. "Come on, William, let's go. Before—"

The orb began to vibrate, like a drum roll.

"What's happening?" Freddy asked, backing away.

"I don't know," William said.

The orb's vibrations increased.

"If it keeps going like that, it's going to punch a hole in the floor," Freddy said.

"Look … it's levitating," Iscia said, wide-eyed.

And, sure enough, the orb rose off the floor and floated upwards. When it reached the height of William's head, it stopped and hovered there in mid-air.

"Let's get out of here," Freddy said and started to go.

"We can't leave it like this," William said.

"Well, switch it off then." Freddy sounded like he was about to cry.

"I don't think that will work," William said.

The orb was vibrating faster and faster, then it let out a high-pitched beeping sound. The noise reminded William of the cannon in Benjamin's lab. Then William felt it. A cold grew in the pit of his stomach and spread through his body, then the stabbing headache began. He knew one of those awful attacks was starting again.

He turned to Iscia. "Get out of here … and get Slapperton."

"Huh?" Iscia didn't understand. "What are you talking about?"

"He said, 'get out of here!'" Freddy shouted and turned to run.

The display cases around them started creaking. William looked down at his feet and realized his body was floating up off the floor.

"Help!" Freddy screamed as he rose up into the air.

"This is bad!" William shouted back. "The orb must somehow be reversing the force of gravity. It's going to destroy everything in here!"

"But the display cases are bolted down," Iscia cried over the noise.

She was hanging upside down, clinging to the edge of one of the cases. William was already floating several metres above the ground and searched in desperation for something to hold on to.

"Get out of here!" he shouted again.

The attack was taking over. He had lost control of his movements and was struggling to remain conscious. It felt like his body was vibrating in time with the orb.

"What's happening William?" he heard Iscia yell.

But William couldn't answer. Everything around him was foggy. He was back in the cave. The floating gold ring vibrated violently and emitted a bright golden light, which shone on the white box on the floor. The vibrations from the hovering ring increased and the box started to levitate upwards towards the hoop then stopped midway.

What had he done?

CHAPTER 20

William tried to gain control of his thoughts. Slowly, things were coming back to him. The old orb … the Depository … weightlessness. He was dizzy and had a terrible headache but he forced his eyes open and looked around. He was lying in a bed, but he wasn't in his room. This room was much bigger and completely white, filled with beds along the walls. The two chauffeur-bots stood guard by a door. William slowly tried to sit up, but jolted back when he saw Goffman standing by a window.

"What happened down there?" Goffman snapped. "Most of the items in the Depository that weren't bolted to the floor were destroyed."

"Destroyed?" William said, confused.

"Yes … destroyed." Goffman stopped by the end of the bed.

"What about Iscia … and Freddy?" William said. "Is Iscia all right?"

"They'll survive," Goffman said. "But there will be consequences for taking you down there."

Goffman leaned his cane against a chair that was next to the bed. He leaned over the bed and stared at William.

"I take it you've found out about Pontus Dippel?" Goffman said.

William nodded.

"I'm sorry we had to keep you in the dark about him … and that I tried to convince you that you were hallucinating," Goffman said. "But that's no excuse for whatever you did to wreck the Depository."

William hung his head in shame. "What happened to Pontus Dippel?" he asked quietly.

"That's what we've been trying to find out," Goffman said. "He's safe in a secret location until he comes round and can tell us who attacked him and how they did it."

"What about the surveillance cameras?" William asked.

"Nothing." Goffman looked up at a surveillance camera on the wall that pointed directly at William's bed. "Whoever it was must have had some kind of scrambling technology."

Goffman nodded to the chauffeurs, who turned and left the room. "Now tell me what happened down there! I need to know what you did to make everything levitate."

William lay there for a moment. "It was down there … in between all the old stuff. I didn't mean—"

"What was down there?" Goffman said.

124

"The orb," William said.

"An orb?" Goffman's eyes opened wide, as if what William had just said frightened him. "There's only one orb kept in the Depository and that was stolen when Pontus was attacked. What did this orb look like?"

"It looked very old and it was quite big – about the size of a basketball." He demonstrated with his hands. "It was covered in scratches and dents."

Goffman just sat in the chair – the little colour he had in his face had drained away. He looked like he had been told that the world was about to end.

"They must have put it back," Goffman mumbled to himself. "And … you activated it?"

William nodded. He was ashamed of himself and annoyed that he had let Freddy talk him into it. William looked down at his hands. He didn't know what to say … or do. It wasn't until now, when it was all quiet, that he heard a faint sound.

Puff … puff … puff.

William gazed around the room. He had thought that he was the only patient in here, but now he saw that the curtains were closed around something in the corner at the other end of the room.

"That sound," William said and looked at Goffman.

"We finally managed to defragment Pontus," Goffman said. "He's in an artificial coma – we're just waiting for him to wake up."

William knew that he had to tell Goffman about the woman with the mechanical hand – he had to at least warn them. He just hoped Goffman would know how to keep Iscia safe.

"There's something else—" William started, but stopped as the door was flung open and Slapperton stormed into the room.

"You're not going to believe this!" he shouted, running towards them.

"What?" Goffman said and got up from the chair.

"I had a suspicion, especially after what William saw after his first attack," Slapperton said, "but during that last wave I pinpointed the source … It's real." His voice trembling with excitement. "It's actually real … and it's been activated."

"What's been activated?" Goffman said.

"The Cryptoportal."

"That's impossible." Goffman stood still for what seemed like for ever. His eyes darted back and forth and finally rested on William. "It all makes sense now… You must have solved the orb and activated the portal."

"What portal?" William asked.

Goffman grabbed Slapperton and started for the door, then turned and looked at William. "You stay here. The guard-bots will keep an eye on you – just don't go anywhere."

Before William knew it, Goffman and Slapperton were gone and two guard-bots had wheeled into the room. William's thoughts raced inside his head.

What was a Cryptoportal?

CHAPTER 21

William couldn't help but feel frustrated at being left behind. Did Goffman expect him to just stay there with everything that was going on? But he had already broken the rules and this time he was determined to listen. William lay back on the bed and thought about the large golden hoop and the box that he had again seen during his attack. He tried to make sense of them, but it only gave him a headache. It was then that it hit him. The smell of burnt rubber.

"William," a hoarse voice said from somewhere in the room.

A paralyzing fear spread through him. William looked around and spotted the woman with the mechanical hand, standing by the window. She grinned and took a step towards him.

"HALT!" both of the guard-bots commanded, raising their passivators.

With a quick push of a button, she evaporated the robots

with a ray from her mechanical hand. She opened a lid on the arm and poured metal dust onto the floor.

"They never learn," she said and pushed another button on the mechanical hand. With a *zap*, she disappeared. William looked around the room. His heart beat feverishly as he sat up further. With another *zap*, the woman reappeared again right at the foot of his bed. William jumped back, making the bed slam into the wall behind him.

"What do you want?" he asked, his voice trembling.

"I've already got what I want." She walked around the bed – her leather boots squeaking with each step. She stopped right next to him and sat down on the edge of the bed. The smell of burnt rubber was unbearable.

"What did you get?" William pushed himself back against the headboard. All he wanted was to move away from her.

"This." The woman held up a leather bag and set it on her lap. She grinned and opened the bag so that he could see inside.

"The orb?" he blurted out. It was the same one that Freddy had shown him in the Depository. The little cockroach scurried across the orb and hid deeper down in the bag.

"The Institute had the orb down there all these years and didn't even know what it was. I stole it from the Depository and I've been trying to break the codes protecting it. But not everyone can be a codebreaking genius like you," she said. "I needed you to solve it for me."

"That's why you chased me outside my school?" William asked.

"Of course," she said. "But then your grandfather brought you back here, so I improvised. I put the orb back where I stole it from – I knew it would be the last place they would look for it – then ... bingo!" She threw out her arms. "I got you to do what I wanted ... right under their noses."

"What does it do?" William asked.

"This orb," she said, tapping the bag with her mechanical hand, "is like a remote control for the Cryptoportal in the Himalayas."

"The Cryptoportal?" William repeated quietly, then he remembered Slapperton talking about a Cryptoportal being activated.

"Those fools at the Institute didn't expect a thing. They thought that the portal was destroyed millions of years ago, but it wasn't." She paused briefly and stared at William with her wild eyes. "And now I'm going to send *him* through it."

"Him?" William asked.

"Well, I might as well tell you ... before I dispose of you." She smiled and pushed a button on her hand. "Although I would have thought that someone with your abilities would have figured it out by now ... I did what they thought was impossible ... what they thought would never happen."

"What?" William said as adrenaline rushed through his body. Was she really going to shoot him?

"During the chaos you created down in the Depository, I took Abraham from the cryogenic chamber." She stood up. "Of course, that was the plan all along, but you only made it easier for me to zap in there and grab him."

William sat there in disbelief. Had she really managed to free Abraham from the escape-proof chamber that he was being held in?

"And now I'm going to send him through the Cryptoportal." She aimed the hand at him. "I'll give him your regards... Goodbye, genius!"

The high-pitched sound from her hand grew stronger, along with a deafening beeping that was so loud William thought his ears would explode. He quickly flung himself off the bed as it was pulverized by a bright beam. He slammed into a cabinet full of medical equipment that fell over and crashed to the floor. Boxes of bandages and rolls of gauze rained down on him. Another ray hit the cabinet and made it disappear in a flash of light.

Without thinking, William threw himself forward and rolled under the curtains around Pontus Dippel's bed. The old man's eyes were closed and he had an oxygen mask over his face. His chest moved in time with the rhythmic puffs from the breathing machine. William took cover behind the bed and looked through the narrow gap between the curtains. Smoke rose from the smouldering pile of metal – the only thing left of the bed he'd been lying in moments before.

"Only babies and cowards hide," he heard the woman say

as her squeaking steps came to a halt right outside the curtain. "You should come out and face me – at least try and keep whatever dignity you have left."

Pontus moaned and stirred. William looked up as the old man blinked and slowly opened his eyes. *No, not now,* William thought as Pontus reached for the oxygen-mask and pulled it away. The old man looked down at William, who put his finger to his mouth, then pointed at the curtains. William could hear a loud beeping as the curtains were flung aside and she appeared – her wild eyes settling on Pontus.

"So this is where you've been hiding." She raised her mechanical hand and grinned. "This is almost too perfect. Two flies in one web."

The old man gasped and threw up his hands. "No, not again," he moaned.

William grabbed hold of Pontus' gown and pulled him off the bed. He landed heavily on the floor and quickly scrambled behind the bed. William looked around – the door was too far away to reach in time.

"*Sayonara,*" the woman said as her lips contorted into a wicked grin and the beeping from her hand increased. William scanned his surroundings for something – anything – he could use to save himself and Pontus from the deadly ray, seconds away from pulverizing them both. His eyes stopped on the leather bag on the floor. The cockroach peeked up from the open zip. Then William had an idea – it was a long shot, but it might just work. He placed his feet on the wall behind him, pushed away as hard as he could and shot forwards. He hit the bed, which crashed into the woman and caused her to stumble backwards. William rolled across the floor and, in one fluid motion, he grabbed the leather bag and hurled it towards the windows.

"NOOOOOOOO!" she screamed.

A pane of glass exploded in a cloud of shards and the orb flew out of the window. The woman lunged after it, like it was the most precious thing in the world. And with a loud *zap*, she and the bag were gone.

William lay still, waiting for her to reappear, but nothing happened. All he could hear was the wailing of an alarm out in the hallway. Slowly, he got to his feet. He looked down at himself to check if he was all there – his legs were shaking, but he was alive.

Suddenly, the door was flung open and a herd of guard-bots rushed through with their passivators ready. They surrounded William as Goffman marched into the ward. He stopped and looked at the destroyed room, then at William.

"I can't leave you alone for a second," Goffman said and shook his head.

"It was her." Pontus Dippel pulled himself up from behind the bed. "It was Cornelia Strangler."

"And she's got Abraham," William said. "She broke him out from the cryogenic chamber."

Goffman's jaw dropped.

CHAPTER 22

The hover-cart raced down the narrow hallways deep below the Institute. William was sitting in the back seat and holding on for dear life, while Slapperton was behind the wheel, with Goffman sat next to him. William had never thought that the hover-cart could travel this fast and the suction from the propeller made his hair flutter. He cast a quick look over his shoulder at the dozen guard-bots that were following them, each one with a passivator in hand.

"I checked the status in the chamber an hour ago," Slapperton shouted over the noise from the fan. "And everything was fine then."

"Could it have happened after that?" Goffman shouted back.

"The system reports no break-in. I can't see how anyone could have got in there, let alone leave with a whole freezer box undetected." Benjamin turned the steering wheel hard, and the hover-craft skidded into another hallway.

133

"She did it when everyone was down at the Depository," William shouted, but the noise from the fan drowned out his voice. The hover-cart came to a screeching halt at the end of a hallway. Slapperton jumped out and stopped in front of an enormous, heavily bolted door.

"Let's get it open," Slapperton said and placed his forehead on a scanner next to the door.

Goffman stepped in front of a scanner on the other side of the door. He leaned in and placed his forehead against it. A faint humming sound came from deep inside the wall and a light over the door changed from red to green.

Slapperton backed up as the iron door started to slide open. The guard-bots gathered in formation and everyone held their breath. A frosty grey mist spilled out from the room and snaked towards them like an enchanted carpet. As soon as the door was open enough to squeeze inside, Slapperton leaped in.

"Wait!" Goffman yelled.

But Slapperton was gone.

"Get in there!" Goffman waved at the guard-bots. "Hurry!"

The guard-bots poured through the door and disappeared inside one after the other. William looked at Goffman, who remained standing still in front of the entrance. It was like he was afraid to go inside – afraid of what might be in there ... or, worse, what wouldn't.

William couldn't stand it any more. He jumped off the hover-cart and pushed past Goffman. He stopped as he entered the room. It was much colder in here and William could see his breath as he exhaled. He looked around and counted a row of ten coffin-like freezers along the wall of the room. William's heart started to beat faster. They were exactly like the one he'd seen under the golden ring in his visions.

Slapperton was in front of an empty space in between the row of freezers. He stood there, motionless – his breath forming puffs of grey frost as he stared at the gap. The guard-bots stood in a semi-circle around him with their passivators raised.

"He's gone," Slapperton said without moving. "I can't believe it… He's actually gone."

CHAPTER 23

Ten minutes later, William was sitting across from Goffman and Pontus in a Rolls-Royce. It was pitch-black outside and the car was moving through the night at tremendous speed. Goffman was digging around in a briefcase, while Pontus sat quietly next to him. Even though it hadn't been long since he had woken up from his artificial coma, Pontus had insisted on coming with them, while Slapperton had decided to stay behind at the Institute and keep monitoring the sound waves.

"Where are we going?" William asked quietly.

"The Institute has a secret airfield close by," Goffman mumbled as he continued to rummage through his briefcase. "A plane is waiting for us there. It's going to take us to the Himalayas."

"The Himalayas?" William gulped.

"Yes," Goffman said and glanced up at William. "According to Benjamin's coordinates that's where the portal is. And with what you saw during your attack, it seems highly likely that he is correct." He looked down at an oversized watch on his wrist. "Eight hours and thirty-seven minutes," he mumbled to himself.

"What kind of watch is that?" William asked and pointed to the device.

Goffman seemed trapped in his own thoughts.

"It's a cryogenic monitor," Pontus said with a raspy voice. "It's linked to Abraham's freezer unit and records different data on the freezer – how cold it is and such." Pontus leaned over and extended his hand. "I'm sorry," he said and smiled. "I don't believe we've been formally introduced."

The old man's hand felt cold as William shook it.

"Pontus Dippel, Curator for the Depository for Impossible Archaeology."

"Yes, I know," William said. "I saw you when you were uh – trapped in that slab of metal."

"Ah, yes," the old man said. "I was lucky. She didn't mean for me to survive, but she was in a hurry. All she cared about was that orb." Pontus paused for a bit and looked at William. "Thank you for saving me in the infirmary, by the way."

"You're welcome." William said.

Pontus turned to Goffman. "Have you found it yet?"

"Here it is." Goffman pulled a faded folder from the brief-case and handed it to William, who took the folder and read the typewritten label on the front.

"Cornelia Strangler?" he said out loud.

"It wasn't until Pontus woke up and confirmed who she was that things started to fall into place." Goffman pointed his bony finger at the folder. "Look inside."

William opened it, and jumped when he saw the picture on the first page. Even though it was an old black and white photograph, he recognized her immediately. It was the woman, staring right at him with piercing, wild eyes.

"She's known as Cornelia Strangler..." Goffman said. "You remember how Abraham Talley was discovered down in the tunnels after he had stumbled upon that lump of luridium? He was then transported from the hospital where he disappeared without a trace a few hours later. It turns out that Cornelia Strangler took him in and tended to him until he was better."

"Why did she help him?" William asked. "Didn't she know that he was a murderer?"

"Strangler isn't her real name. She changed it from something else..." Pontus said. "Her real last name is ... Talley."

"She's his daughter," Goffman said.

William's mouth fell open. He didn't know what to say.

"But the real kicker is," Pontus said, "that she died an old woman, in the twentieth century." Pontus fell silent, like he wanted to give William time to process the information. "And she has remained dead until she showed up now, at the Institute. Not only has she come back from the dead, but somehow, she seems to have made herself younger."

"How can that be possible?" William asked, looking down at the photo again.

"We don't know," Goffman said, shrugging. "It's a mystery."

"Abraham stopped ageing when the luridium got inside him," William said. "Could the same have happened to her?"

"For that to happen," Goffman said, "you would need to be almost a hundred per cent luridium, like Abraham."

"And now she's managed to get away with the entire cryonic storage unit – including the cooling elements, nitrogen container and Abraham Talley inside – right under our noses," Pontus wiped his nose with a handkerchief and glanced over at Goffman.

"How?" William said.

"That mechanical hand of hers must have a very powerful defragmentation drive." Goffman paused for a bit. "It enables her to rip the atoms in any material object apart, and reassemble it again in a different place."

"In simpler words," Pontus said, "it's a portable teleportation device. That's what she shot me with in the Depository."

"You stumbled upon Pontus when we were preparing to free him," Goffman said. "We wanted to wait until Benjamin had found the reason for your attacks before we told you what we knew. That's why we moved Pontus to the infirmary."

They sat in silence for a while. William looked out of the car window at the darkness. It was dawning on him that he had helped Cornelia activate that Cryptoportal and free Abraham from the Institute.

"So, Abraham is on the loose again," William said.

"In a way," Goffman said, glancing down at his watch. "But he's still frozen."

"For however long that lasts." Pontus shot Goffman a quick glance.

"Cornelia used you to activate the portal," Goffman said. "And you're the only one who can deactivate it. We have to get to the portal in the Himalayas and stop her before she manages to send Abraham through it."

"How are we going to do that?" William said.

"There will be a full briefing on the plane." Goffman leaned over and tapped his cane on the glass to alert the chaffeur-bots. William tipped back in his seat as the car picked up speed.

CHAPTER 24

The Rolls-Royce went through a set of gates and continued onto a large runway. It was dark outside, other than the light coming from the headlights on the car. The vehicle came to a halt and Goffman opened the door.

"Let's go," he said and stepped out. "The plane will be here any moment."

"Good luck," Pontus said and stayed seated.

"You're not coming?" William asked.

"I wish I could, but my health isn't what it used to be – and being stuck in a hunk of metal for days hasn't exactly helped. I've told them all I know, so now it's time for me to leave."

William gave the old man a reassuring smile, before he climbed out of the car and closed the door behind him. As he watched the car drive off he noticed the two chauffeur-bots were standing on the runway.

"It can drive by itself?" William asked Goffman as the car disappeared into the darkness.

"Of course," Goffman said.

"So you don't need the chauffeurs?" William said.

"Not for driving the car." Goffman smiled. "But they like it in the front, and they come in handy for so many other things."

The two chauffeurs positioned themselves out in the field. One of them turned the passivator torch on, pointing the beam of light up into the starlit night. William and Goffman watched the sky but, every now and then, Goffman would glance at the cryogenic counter strapped to his wrist. Finally, there was a distant hum.

"Here they come," Goffman said as a gigantic aeroplane materialized in the black sky above them, approaching at high speed.

"Where's it going to land?" William asked.

"It's not," Goffman replied.

William stood spellbound, staring at the huge white plane that hovered in the air above them. It was as long as a football field, shaped like an enormous whale and it didn't have any windows – not even where the pilots would usually sit. Suddenly a hatch opened from the bottom of the plane and a platform lowered down in front of them.

"Come on," Goffman said and stepped onto it.

*   *   *

William, Goffman and the two chauffeurs were standing in a large cargo hold inside the plane.

"The plane will take us to the Himalayas," Goffman shouted over the hum of the powerful engines. "We're prepared for most eventualities. That device over there, for example, is a snowmobile." Goffman pointed to a machine the size of a small tractor that had a glass roof and belts instead of wheels. "And those are the escape pods over there," Goffman said, nodding at two glass spheres sitting in front of a large door in the wall.

"Glass escape pods?" William said. "That seems like a strange choice of material."

"Shatter-resistant glass," Goffman said.

"And what are those?" William asked, pointing to a row of grey jumpsuits hanging along the wall.

"The latest prototype of our Ultra-suits. We're very proud of this model," Goffman said. "They're made of material that changes attributes depending on the circumstances. Even the soles on the bottom of the boots adapt to the surface you're walking on."

William ran his fingers over the material. He could feel it changing texture under his touch. "Cool," he whispered to himself. "It's as if it's alive."

"Welcome, Mr Goffman," a voice said from behind them.

William turned around and saw a square robot about the size of a milk crate that had a big, ball-like eye.

"I'll show you to your rooms. The briefing is in T-minus

143

thirty-four minutes," the strange box-shaped robot continued. "Follow me."

Goffman and William followed the robot as it hobbled away.

"Now that I have you here—" the robot looked up at Goffman with its big eye—"there are a couple of things I'd like to discuss with you."

"Yes?" Goffman said.

"I'm tired of not having a real name," the robot said. "And I'm tired of all the nicknames: Boxer, Square Pants, Crate … et cetera."

"For the time being, we'll call you Beta – that will have to do. You haven't even been patented yet," Goffman said. "And you're still not completely finished."

"If I might suggest a change," Beta said, "a round shape might be more practical, then I could roll instead of bump, and I would get cool nicknames like Bounce, Globe or Speedball."

"We'll see," Goffman said and then turned to William. "You have your own compartment. I recommend that you get some rest. We'll have a briefing on the situation soon and we arrive in a few hours – Beta will show you the way."

"Follow me," Beta said, clattering away across the metal floor like a clumsy die.

William stepped into a spacious compartment and looked around. There was a bed, a small sofa, a desk and a flat-screen TV on the wall that showed clouds moving in a blue sky.

William walked over to the screen and looked closer.

"The plane doesn't have any windows, so each room has a screen that shows you what's going on outside," Beta said. "Not being able to see outside causes some people to feel claustrophobic, so the screens help."

"Cool," William said.

"It gets cooler. In five minutes we'll be leaving the atmosphere and entering space."

"Space?" William said, staring back at the robot.

"Yup," Beta said. "We'll go a lot faster without the air resistance, we'll be travelling in a vacuum. Conventional planes take twelve hours, but we'll be there in a little under two."

"Wow!" William said, impressed, and glanced at the flat screen again. It was showing the blue sky darkening as they rose over the earth's atmosphere.

"I'll collect you for the briefing in thirty minutes," Beta informed him and backed out of the room.

William sat on the bed and put his face in his hands. Abraham Talley was on the loose again and now, they were chasing him to the Himalayas. It felt like a bad dream. How could he have allowed himself to be tricked into solving the orb? He'd been so stupid. From now on, he was going to be more alert – more vigilant. If he was the reason for the mess that they were in, then he would have to be the one to get them out of it.

CHAPTER 25

Thirty minutes later, William was jogging down a narrow hallway behind the square robot, which clunked to a halt outside a white door. The door opened with a soft *swoosh* and they continued into the plane's canteen. Goffman was standing by a table at the end of the room, where two people were already seated with their backs to William.

Iscia turned around and smiled at him. William hadn't seen her since the disaster at the Depository for Impossible Archaeology. She seemed fine – at last, some good news – William breathed a sigh of relief.

"Iscia! What are you doing here?" he asked, smiling.

"What do you think?" she said smiling back. "We're here to help."

The person sitting next to her turned around and looked at him. A mixture of feelings bubbled up inside William. He was so glad to see Iscia that he had forgotten all about Freddy.

"Come and have a seat," Goffman said, gesturing for William to sit down.

William walked over to the only free chair, right next to Freddy. He hesitated. Freddy was the one who goaded him into solving the orb in the first place and William was beginning to wonder whether he could trust him. Freddy suddenly stood up and held out his hand.

"William, it's so nice to see you. And sorry about what happened in the Depository ... if I had any idea what that orb was capable of, I wouldn't have gone near it."

"That's OK," was all William managed to say.

"Shake his hand then!" Iscia whispered and nudged William with her elbow.

He took Freddy's hand and they shook.

"Have a seat," Freddy said, pulling the chair out for him.

Goffman took a remote control out of his pocket and pushed one of the buttons. A hologram of a golden ring covered in strange symbols appeared in the air right above the tabletop and rotated slowly. William recognized it immediately – it was the same golden ring he'd seen during his attacks.

"According to the old, secret texts at the Institute as well as William's description of his visions, this is what we believe the Cryptoportal looks like." Goffman paused, took a sip of water from a glass on the table, cleared his throat and continued. "We thought that the Cryptoportal had been destroyed millions of years ago. That was until William accidently solved an orb at the Depository for Impossible Archaeology and, somehow, remotely brought the portal back."

William swallowed. "Again, I'm so—" He stopped himself mid-sentence. He felt so bad for what he had done and there was nothing he could say to make it better.

"What does the portal do?" Iscia asked.

William was grateful that she had taken the attention off him.

Goffman scratched his chin as he watched the rotating hologram. "We don't know that much about it but, according to the texts, it was used to evacuate humankind from Earth a long time ago and, with it, luridium."

"How long ago?" William asked.

"Again, according to the texts," Goffman said, "it happened right before the Karoo Ice Age, which started around three hundred and sixty million years ago."

"And there weren't people on Earth that long ago," William added.

"Not according to mainstream science," Goffman said. "But all three of you have seen those impossible objects at the Depository, and we now know from the texts that intelligent, human-like beings made the portal before the Karoo Ice Age."

"Which means that it's older than three hundred and sixty million years?" Iscia said.

"Correct." Goffman nodded.

"But how is the portal connected to what has been happening at the Institute?" Iscia asked.

"From what she told William, it seems that Cornelia's plan is to send Abraham through the portal."

"But isn't that a good thing?" Freddy asked. "If she sends him away, we won't have to worry about him any more."

"I wish it were that simple, Freddy," Goffman said. "We believe that ever since Abraham's body was invaded by luridium, he's been working to bring luridium back to Earth. We think this behaviour is programmed into the luridium itself, making Abraham act on behalf of it."

"Programmed?" William asked. "How?"

"When luridium enters a living body, the information programmed into it invades the brain of the infected and takes over. It's like transferring data."

"Like mind control?"

"Yes – well, more like stealth mind control, since the victim is unaware that they are being controlled by a programme."

"So why doesn't the luridium control William?" Iscia said and looked over at him.

"It seems that it doesn't affect William in the same way – perhaps because his body is made up of less luridium," Goffman said. "That's why your grandfather made sure to only inject you with forty-nine per cent luridium. If he'd gone over that, you might have been a very different boy. Instead, the luridium simply makes your innate codebreaking talent stronger."

"So," Iscia continued, "there's no danger of this happening to William, since he's only forty-nine per cent luridium?"

"There's always a danger." Goffman looked at William. "But it seems that you have a naturally high resistance to luridium and I think that if you happened to get more into your body, it may even enhance your abilities – but that's only speculation; we can't be sure."

Iscia folded her arms over her chest and shot William a concerned look, as if she didn't fully buy Goffman's explanation. The group sat in silence for a few seconds.

"Where does the portal lead?" William asked, trying to take the focus off himself.

"We don't know for sure and can only speculate," Goffman said. "But, judging by the texts, it leads to a different dimension."

"So she's going to send Abraham to a different dimension? Why?" Freddy asked.

"According to the information the Institute has gathered, it seems that a long time ago, there were intelligent beings on Earth that invented luridium."

"Humans?" Iscia shot in.

"Yes, humans," Goffman replied, scratching his chin. "But the luridium turned against them and took over their bodies. We think that the luridium destroyed almost all life here and then it used the portal to evacuate earth right before a great ice age." Goffman paused and gave the others a serious nod.

"As I understand it, the only thing that weakens luridium is extreme cold, which would explain why it wanted to leave Earth before then."

"That also explains why Abraham was cryogenically frozen at the Institute," William said.

"Correct," Goffman said. "The cold shuts down his powers. We need to ensure that he remains frozen – otherwise Cornelia will send him through the portal once he regains his power."

"But what happens if he's sent through?" Iscia asked.

"We don't know for sure," Goffman said, his face twitching nervously. "But we can't take any chances. We know that Abraham wants to bring luridium back to earth and…"

"And?" William said.

Goffman snapped back into the present and looked at William. "And – worst-case scenario – the luridium will return to Earth and finish the job of infecting all humans. It will invade and conquer the planet… In short, we'd all be doomed."

"So, we have to find Cornelia and stop her from using the portal," William said.

"Correct." Goffman looked at William. "And as you know, you're the only one who has the codebreaking skills to deactivate it."

William nodded. He would do whatever he had to do to stop Cornelia.

"There's just one problem," Goffman continued, "we don't quite know how you will react to being so close to the portal…

It's the portal that has been causing your attacks, William."

"The portal?" William said, shocked.

"Yes," Goffman said. "Benjamin got a clear reading when you solved the orb at the Depository. It turns out that the sound waves that have been causing your attacks are being emitted by the portal."

"So, every time I've had an attack, it was because of the Cryptoportal?" William asked.

Goffman nodded. "The portal has been dormant for all these years, but since Cornelia stole the orb from the Depository, she's been trying to activate it. She solved some of the codes and the portal started emitting bursts of signals. Since you're more human than luridium, it affects you like it affected the cockroach that Benjamin had in his lab."

"So what do we do when we get to the Himalayas?" William asked.

"We meet up with your grandfather – he's been there since he dropped you off at the Institute," Goffman said.

"He has?" William almost shouted. With all that had happened in the past couple of days he'd barely had time to think about his grandfather.

"Yes," Goffman said, smiling. "Benjamin has been guiding him and trying to locate the source of the signals. It's been a struggle, but when you solved the orb at the Depository, they pinpointed the source of the signal and your grandfather found an entrance to an ancient underground system in the mountains. The plan is to meet up with him there and try to close the portal."

William felt a sudden surge of relief. Now, he understood why his grandfather had left him so suddenly – it wasn't because he didn't care about him, he just had much more serious matters to take care of.

Goffman gave William a stern look. "Your grandfather will take us down into the system where the portal is, but William, you're the only one who can deactivate the portal and Cornelia will stop at nothing to prevent you from doing so." Goffman paused. "Do you think you can handle it?"

William nodded. He had to.

CHAPTER 26

When William got back to his room, it hit him that he was going to the Himalayas, where Cornelia Strangler and Abraham Talley – the people he feared most – were waiting. Only he could prevent Cornelia from sending Abraham through the Cryptoportal, the same portal that triggered William's severe attacks and caused him to lose control over his own body. Suddenly, the situation seemed hopeless.

The image on the flat screen was gradually turning from black to blue and William realized that the plane must be descending. There was a knock on the door. It opened and Iscia poked her head in.

"Are you busy?" she asked.

"No," William said and got up. "Come inside." He was glad to see her.

"You got a bigger room than me," she said as she stepped inside and sat down on the bed. She rocked back and forth as if testing the mattress. "A nicer bed, too."

William didn't know what to say. How could she be talking about rooms and beds at a time like this?

"I like this plane," Iscia said, smiling. "Too bad we won't be on it longer."

They sat gazing around the room for a few seconds.

"How are you doing?" she asked, glancing at him.

"Fine," he lied.

"You almost destroyed the entire Depository at the Institute," Iscia said. "I can't believe they didn't have you cryogenically frozen!"

"Goffman wasn't as mad as I thought he would be," William said.

"That's because he has his hands full right now," Iscia said. "Plus … he knows that he needs your skills."

William nodded. The plane shook and Iscia held on to the bed.

"Turbulence," William murmured as he looked towards the screen on the wall. It showed a wide mountain chain far below them – they were approaching the Himalayas.

"It's beautiful," Iscia said. "Have you been here before?"

"No." William shook his head. "You?"

"Never, but I've always wanted to go."

Iscia grabbed the bed and held on as the plane shook again. It felt like they were sliding down a snowy hill on a large sledge.

"I hate turbulence," she said, looking at the TV again.

"The weather seems fine out there. Why are we hopping around like this?"

"There can be turbulence in nice weather too," William said. "It's harmless … where's Freddy?"

"In his room." Iscia shrugged. "He said he has a headache, but he's been acting pretty strange ever since the incident in the Depository."

"Strange?" William said. "How?"

"Don't know really. He just seems a bit nervous." She looked at William. "What do you make of all that stuff Goffman told us?"

"I'm still trying to work it all out," William said.

"Yeah," Iscia shrugged. "It made me think of an old roll of parchment that I read once in the Depository. It talked about an advanced civilization disappearing from earth millions of years ago." She shot him an inquisitive look. "Could that have been the same civilization that Goffman was talking about?"

William shrugged. "Maybe. If there was an advanced civilization on earth before us, and they invented something so intelligent like luridium, it could have turned on them and taken over their bodies." William paused; it was a scary thought.

"Almost like where humanity is now," Iscia said, "with robots and all of our advanced technology."

The plane shook as they hit more turbulence.

"Are you relieved that they found out what's been triggering your attacks?"

"In a way," William said, fidgeting.

"Only in a way?" she said.

"Well … we're on our way to the source of the attacks right now," William said and looked at his hands.

Iscia's face grew serious. She was about to say something but the plane shook again and this time the shaking increased. An alarm started wailing out in the hallway.

"What's going on?" Iscia said and tried to get to her feet.

William staggered towards the door that Iscia had already opened and saw Beta on its way past.

"It's mild turbulence," Beta's flat voice stated. "Nothing to worry about."

"This is more than turbulence," William said.

"There's also a slight problem with the electrical system on the plane," Beta said.

"What sort of problem?" William asked.

They were suddenly flung up against the ceiling. William desperately tried to grip on to the flat surface with his hands as he was pinned to the ceiling right next to Iscia.

"Nothing to worry about," Beta repeated. "Only a little free fall. It'll be over soon."

"Look!" Iscia shouted and used all of her strength to point to something on the wall in the hallway below them. "What's that?"

A spider-like shadow jumped out from a small box in the wall. A sign on the inside of the open case read: *fuse-box.*

There was a loud *pop* from the box and sparks flew out like a fire cracker had exploded. The spider-shadow landed on the floor and scurried along the hallway towards them, but as it passed under them, William recognized it. It was Cornelia Strangler's mechanical hand. The device was somehow moving around on its own.

"Cornelia's on the plane!" William shouted, watching as the hand sped down the hallway and disappeared around a corner. The plane shook again and they crashed to the floor.

"We have to find the others!" William shouted as he scrambled to his feet and grabbed Iscia. "This way!" he yelled, pulling her down the hallway as the lights on the plane went out.

"I can't see anything!" Iscia shouted over the noise from the screaming engines.

"Emergency power generator activated," Beta said from right behind them and a red light came on in the ceiling.

"Beta! Where are the others?" Iscia shouted.

"One moment..." Beta said. "The others are on their way to the escape pods – you should go there too. The plane's auto-pilot is flying, and we'll be making an uncontrolled controlled emergency landing."

"UNCONTROLLED?!" William shot Beta a startled look. "You told me there was nothing to worry about!"

"Would you care for a little calming music to soothe the nerves?" Beta asked.

"While we're waiting to crash?" William shouted.

Piano music poured out of a little speaker on the front of the box-shaped robot. Iscia looked at William, her eyes wide with fear. They staggered down the hallway and stopped at a door with a sign that said in big, green letters: *To the escape pods*. Iscia pushed on the door handle, but it was locked. The plane jerked so violently that it was almost impossible for them to stay upright.

"Beta, can you open it?!" William shouted over the deafening noise and classical music.

"One moment…" Beta said.

The whole body of the plane started to tilt forwards, its walls shaking so much that William was afraid that it would tear apart at any moment. The drone of the engines increased even more as Iscia desperately clung on to the door handle.

"Beta?!" William shouted again.

The door suddenly opened with a soft *click* and they all stumbled through it and down the stairs.

"Uncontrolled controlled emergency landing in T-minus three minutes," Beta said.

"This way," Iscia yelled pointing to the entrance of the cargo hold as a powerful gust of wind tore at their clothes.

"Uncontrolled controlled emergency landing in T-minus two and a half minutes," Beta announced.

William and Iscia stumbled into the cargo hold and saw Goffman, Freddy and one of the chauffeurs next to the two escape pods. They were struggling to get into their Ultra-suits, but Goffman's face filled with relief when he spotted William and Iscia.

"You made it!" he shouted. "Hurry up and put on your suits! We have to get into the escape pods before the plane hits the ground!" Goffman took down two Ultra-suits and tossed them to William and Iscia. The plane shook again, making the escape pods sway.

"Uncontrolled controlled emergency landing in T-minus two minutes," Beta said, bobbing in through the door and filling the room with soothing piano music. William struggled to get his Ultra-suit on – it was like putting on a wetsuit. The second chauffeur came in through the door and opened the hatch to the escape pods. Goffman, Freddy and both chauffeurs jumped in and William hobbled towards the pod, even though he hadn't managed to get his Ultra-suit on all the way yet.

"Come on!" William shouted, waving at Iscia who was also still fighting to get her suit on.

"Uncontrolled controlled emergency landing in T-minus thirty seconds," Beta said.

"Get in here now!" Goffman shouted, sticking his head out of the pod's door and frantically waving at them.

The plane shook so violently that William and Iscia fell to the ground. When William lifted his head, he saw that the escape pod with Goffman and the others had broken free and was on its way out through the open doorway.

"No … wait!" he shouted.

"Look out!" Iscia screamed.

William threw himself to the side just as a snowmobile skidded towards the open door and collided with the escape pod outside. He got to his feet and saw Goffman's terror-stricken face staring back at him from the escape pod as it tumbled into the snowy chaos below.

"Uncontrolled controlled emergency landing in T-minus ten seconds," Beta said.

"We have to get in the other pod!" William shouted, pointing to the second escape pod.

They both sprinted to the pod and jumped inside. William quickly pulled the door shut behind them and sat down into the seat, where a seatbelt shot out and secured him in. The pod had ten seats along the wall and a red lever sticking out of the middle of the floor. He nodded at Iscia, who was also secured in her seat beside him, and pulled the lever. The escape pod started to roll towards the door. William cast one last look back as they bounced out into the storm. His stomach lurched as he spotted a figure standing in the empty room.

It was Cornelia. She grinned at him as her mechanical hand scurried across the floor and jumped towards her. Cornelia caught it and screwed it back in place, then slowly raised her mechanical hand and waved at him.

"Have a nice death," her voice somehow said from inside William's head and, with a burst of light, she was gone.

CHAPTER 27

Stop it! thought William. He lifted his hand and wiped his face, trying to brush away whatever was stinging him. A wave of intense cold surged through his body as he slowly came round. He tried to open his eyes but it felt like they were frozen shut and when he finally managed to force them open, he saw that he was lying in an endless ocean of white snow. The howling wind whipped his face and his fingers were numb.

He had to get out of the cold before it was too late – he had to start moving and warm up again. William put his hands over his face and blew to try to warm up his cheeks, which were frozen stiff, but he was so cold that the air coming out of his mouth felt like ice. He struggled up onto his knees and looked around for any sign of the others, but it was snowing heavily and he could barely see in front of him. They must have crashed somewhere deep in the Himalayas.

Then William felt warmth spreading through his body and

he realized that the Ultra-suit was heating up. A small red light on the suit started blinking and he watched as gloves grew out of the sleeve and covered his hands. In a flash, a hood had risen up from the collar and formed around his head, leaving only his face exposed. His breathing calmed down and he felt his strength returning. Now that he was warming up he could think clearly again – he had to find the others.

"ISCIAAAAA?!" he shouted, but his voice was drowned out by the howling wind around him. William started moving through the waist-deep snow, using his arms to dig his way forward. He stopped and looked around in despair and then he spotted something a little way off – something half-buried in the snow. William squinted into the wind. It was the escape pod. He fought his way over to the glass shell that was half covered in snow and looked inside. It was empty.

"IIIIISCIIIIIAAAAAA!" he called again, scanning the horizon. If she had started walking, then the snow would have covered her tracks. William took another look at the pod. Should he seek shelter inside and wait for help? But what if Iscia was trapped out there in the storm or lying somewhere, unconscious and freezing to death?

Then he saw it: a red light, blinking in the white distance. It was difficult to judge how far away it was but it pulsated with three long bursts and three short bursts. William knew that meant SOS – the international code for distress. He peered down at the light on his chest that blinked with the same rhythm. There was someone in the storm, someone with an Ultra-suit like his. It had to be one of the other passengers from the plane.

The light disappeared. William fixed his gaze on the spot where it had been, hoping that it might return. He started walking again, fighting his way through the snow and gritting his teeth to steel himself. Every step was a struggle as his legs sank further into the snow, but he had to keep moving in the direction where the light had been. He caught a glimpse of something in all the whiteness ahead of him – a dark fleck. As he moved closer, the contours of a mountain appeared and he realized that the shape was the mouth of a cave. Soon he was standing at the snow covered entrance, peering into the darkness ahead.

"Hello?"

The only response was his echo and the howling wind behind him. As he moved further in, it became increasingly difficult to see, but then a beam of light shot out from the top of his suit. It seemed that the Ultra-suit also had a built-in, automatic torch and the narrow beam gave out just enough light for William to be able to see in front of him.

"Hello?" he said again as he walked.

The howling from the storm outside grew quieter and water dripped from the roof of the cave and hit the ground, making the floor slick and wet. He could feel the bottom of his boots changing with each step he took, sucking his feet to the ground. William stopped as the red light blinked in the darkness in front of him.

"Hello?" William said again.

There was no reply. He aimed his flashlight at the red light, but it was just beyond the beam's reach. As he got closer, he could make out the contours of a body, suspended a couple of metres above the ground. And then he realized who it was. Her eyes were closed, and her head was tilted forwards.

"Iscia!" he shouted and ran towards her.

The air in front of William suddenly crackled and he was flung backwards. It was like being hit by an invisible wall and he landed hard on his back on the stone ground.

"ISCIA!" William coughed and tried to sit up.

"She can't hear you," a hoarse voice said from inside his head. William looked around and spotted the dark shadow further back in the cave.

"What did you do to her?"

"I saved her," Cornelia said, walking into the beam of light. "You should thank me."

"Thank you? I heard your voice in my head when the plane crashed – you tried to kill me."

"But now you're here anyway," Cornelia said. "You're a hard one to get rid of." She took a step closer and bared her yellow teeth in a sort of sneer. "You shouldn't have come here. I'm afraid that you're going to pay for it."

There was something animal-like about her – as if she was

more wolf than human – and her eyes almost glowed. William looked around for a rock or something that he could use as a weapon. His body tensed as he prepared for battle – he wasn't going to let Cornelia harm Iscia.

"Don't touch her!" William yelled as Cornelia walked over to her.

He ran towards them, slamming into the invisible wall again. For a second time, he was flung backwards and landed on the ground, but he quickly got to his feet. Cornelia raised her mechanical hand, pushed a button and shot a beam of light that hit him in the chest. William's body stiffened completely and he stood there, unable to move. It was as if an invisible force was holding him up. Was there no end to what Cornelia could do with her mechanical hand? She took a step towards William and leaned in so close that her nose almost touched his. Her breath stank of burnt rubber and the fumes stung his eyes.

"Why are you doing this?" William asked. "Don't you know what Abraham is capable of?"

"Of course I know," Cornelia snickered. "I'm finishing what my grandmother started."

"Your *grandmother*?" William repeated. "They said that you were his *daughter* – that you died and came back somehow."

Cornelia laughed hard. "They think that I came back from the dead? Those stupid people!" She stopped laughing and set her glowing eyes on him. "I'm the third generation. My grandmother was his daughter – when she died, my mother took over and then me after her."

"There have been three of you?" William said, surprised.

"I'm Cornelia Strangler the Third," she said with a proud smile. "Born to serve Abraham." Her eyes flickered madly when she said Abraham's name, then she pushed her face even closer to William's – her rancid breath making it difficult for him to breathe.

"I'm going to complete what my grandmother and mother set out to do," she said with a proud smile. "I'm going to send him through the portal."

"Do you realize what could happen if you do?" William asked.

"Of course," she said through clenched teeth. "The Earth belongs to those who left … now it's ripe again for them to return … and Abraham Talley is going to bring them back."

"You're crazy," William said. He tried to wiggle free from the invisible force that was holding him, but he was stuck. He fought the urge to look away – he wouldn't give her the satisfaction of showing that he was afraid.

Cornelia raised her mechanical hand and held it up in front of his face. "I could end you both here and now," she said, her dry lips twisting. "But you've got a lot of fight in you and Abraham could use someone like that … and, since you're already here with those fools from the Institute, you might come in handy."

William blinked. *What was she talking about?*

"Here's what you're going to do," she said, pressing her cold mechanical fist into his face. "Don't say anything about our little meeting to those other idiots ... but when you get to the portal, you're going to help me. Only then will you see your little girlfriend again."

"Help you?" William said. "How?"

"By not doing anything." Cornelia grinned. "They think you're going to deactivate the portal and you will pretend that you are trying ... but, you will do nothing. If you tell them anything or mention seeing me here—" she pointed at Iscia—"she's gone for ever. When they ask you where she is, you'll say that you got separated in the crash."

William felt some kind of energy emitting from the mechanical hand – like a cold fog slowly creeping into his mind. He tried to fight it, but he couldn't think clearly. Was it some kind of mind control?

"OK," William whispered and felt his heart sink. She had him. It was the perfect plan and he knew that he didn't have any other choice than to play along. Cornelia pulled back her fist and straightened up. Her piercing eyes were still trained on him.

"And there's one more thing," she said.

William looked at her, dreading what was coming next.

"When Abraham is through the portal—" she paused— "you're going through it after him. You two are made of the same stuff – you belong with him."

She suddenly pointed her mechanical hand at William and fired. The ray hit him with so much force that he hurtled through the air.

CHAPTER 28

William opened his eyes. He must have landed heavily in the snow and he realized that he had couldn't feel his arms. He desperately tried to move them so that he could dig his way out, but it was no use. He was trapped, face down, in a thick layer of snow and he was starting to feel like he couldn't breathe.

"It's William!" he heard a voice shout.

William felt someone grab his feet and slowly pull him free from the snow. One of the chauffeur-bots helped him up and urged him towards a vehicle. He recognized the snowmobile from the cargo hold and his legs trembled as he climbed in and sat down. Goffman hopped into the seat in front of him and shut the door.

"We've been looking for you everywhere. We thought you had—" he began, but cut himself short. "Where's Iscia?"

William wanted to tell him everything – about Cornelia and her plan – but he couldn't risk anything happening to Iscia.

"She's not with you?" Goffman looked startled.

"No." William shook his head.

"But you must have been with her when the plane crashed." Goffman said. "Didn't you see what happened to her?"

"I hit my head," William said. "When I came to, she was gone. So was the plane."

"The plane is equipped with a chameleon generator. It activates in emergency situations and makes the plane invisible." Goffman looked out at the snow whipping the windscreen. "We have to find her." He pointed at one of the chauffeurs. "Go and look for her."

The chauffeur nodded, turned and disappeared into the white storm. Freddy stared at William with narrowed eyes.

"If she's out there, the chauffeur will find her," Goffman said. "And her Ultra-suit will protect her in the meantime. The most important thing now is that we get to the portal." Goffman paused and looked at his cryogenic counter. He nodded to the chauffeur behind the wheel and the snowmobile moved off again.

Some while later, the vehicle stopped.

"This is it," Goffman said, looking at the coordinates on the GPS screen in front of him.

William looked out of the window, but all he could see was white.

"There's nothing out there," Freddy said.

"Look up." Goffman pointed to the glass roof in the ceiling.

High above them was a temple surrounded by a blizzard of white snow. Slowly William could make out the contours of a mountain around the building, and as he raised his gaze even more, he saw the ragged edges of the top of a mountain. The temple had been built in the middle of a rock face.

"According to the coordinates," Goffman said, "the entrance is through that convent up there."

"Why did they build a convent in the middle of a mountainside?" Freddy asked.

"It was common back then," Goffman said. "The elevation made it easier to defend against attackers."

"Do we have to climb up there?" Freddy asked.

"No," Goffman said and waved at the chauffeur behind the wheel.

The android pressed a button and the snowmobile slowly rose from the ground. William looked out of the window and saw long metal legs extending from both sides of the vehicle. They reminded him of the crab he had made for his school project.

"It's biomimetics – a lot of our research at the Institute is related to this field. The exoskeleton of the snowmobile is inspired by beetles, and we based the extending legs on crab legs," Goffman said. "Fasten your seatbelts – it's going to get bumpy."

The whole vehicle tipped backwards as the front legs

grabbed hold of the rock face and started climbing. The snowmobile shook as the mechanical legs carried them higher and higher. William peered down at the icy ground far below. He had never been fond of heights, but falling was the least of his worries now. He looked over at Freddy, who was clinging to the seat in front of him, fear visible in his wide eyes. The snowmobile jerked as one of the legs lost its grip and they tilted to the side. Freddy screamed, fell out of his seat and crashed into the glass wall.

"Seatbelt!" Goffman shouted.

"I forgot," Freddy cried, crawling into the nearest seat.

The snowmobile regained its grip and continued the ascent up the steep mountainside. A few nerve-racking minutes later, they reached the ledge outside the monastery and the snow-mobile came to a halt.

"Everyone out," Goffman said and opened the door. "We don't have much time."

William followed the others and stepped out onto the ledge. It seemed to be protected from the wind and snow and he could now see the monastery in every detail. It looked like a Tibetan temple, only much older than the ones William had seen in photos of similar temples. The roof tiles were dark green and the stone walls glimmered with something that shone like gold.

"Where is Tobias?" Goffman said and glanced down at his watch. "He said he would meet us here."

"You made it!" a familiar voice said.

William turned and saw a ragged figure coming down the monastery steps. His hair and beard were scruffy, his clothes were dirty and a passivator hung limply from a strap over his shoulder.

"Grandad!" William shouted, wading through the snow as Tobias Wenton opened his arms and ushered him forwards. William clung to him as he fought back tears and the lump growing in his throat. He wanted so badly to tell his grandfather about Cornelia and her plan to send William through the portal, but he knew he couldn't risk Iscia's life.

His grandfather patted him on the back and pulled him towards the monastery. "Come … we'll talk on the way."

The small group continued up the stairs and in through the gilded doors. The only light inside came from a fire in the middle of the empty hall. The monastery had clearly been abandoned a long time ago and as William adjusted his eyes to the dark, he saw figures hunched over the fire. There were three of them, and each had large furs draped over their shoulders.

"They're Sherpas," his grandfather said and stopped next to William. "They've been helping me search for the entrance, but they refuse to go inside. It's something to do with an old myth."

"What myth?" William asked without taking his eyes off the Sherpas.

"That anyone who goes into the sacred caves will never

return," Grandfather said and forced a smile.

"Was this place built by the same people who made luridium?" William asked.

"This monastery is millions of years old," Grandfather said, "but the portal is even older, and I think that this monastery was built by people of a much more recent date. They must have found the portal and thought that it was a gate to the underworld and built all of this around it."

William nodded.

"Come," his grandfather said, and continued into the cave.

The group stopped in front of a round brass door that stood slightly ajar. It looked like the door was divided into smaller pieces that could be moved. William ran his fingers over the strange symbols covering the surface.

"The door is protected by codes," his grandfather said. "It took me a while, but I finally cracked them." He pushed the door open to reveal a small room on the other side.

"A lift?" William said.

"Yes," his grandfather replied. "Isn't it amazing? Those ancient ones had a knack for technology."

They all stepped into the lift and the door slid shut behind them. William looked up at a glass sphere in the ceiling that glowed green from the inside.

"There are some things we know about the civilization that made this stuff," his grandfather said, "from old texts we have at the Institute." He pointed at the lamp. "They called it Opal gas. It comes from deep inside the earth and it seems to be charged by some kind of electricity. The gas provides most of the lighting down here – it must have lasted for eons.

William glanced over at Freddy, who was fidgeting nervously. Iscia had been right – Freddy was acting strange.

"How are you doing?" Tobias said, turning to William. "Did they manage to get your attacks under control?"

"Not entirely," William answered.

"Oh?" his grandfather looked at Goffman. He hesitated a bit before continuing. "Are you sure it's Cornelia?"

"Yes," Goffman said with a serious nod.

"How is that possible?"

Goffman shrugged. "We don't know."

William wanted to tell them that Cornelia was the third generation – Cornelia the Third – and she hadn't come back from the dead; she had been alive all along. But he knew that if he did, he would have to tell them about the meeting in the cave and that would put Iscia at risk. The group stood in silence for a little while as the lift continued to move.

"Where's Iscia?" Tobias asked.

"She went missing in the snowstorm," Goffman said. "One of the chauffeurs is out looking for her."

"Is she wearing an Ultra-suit?"

"Yes," Goffman said.

"That's good, she'll be all right then." Tobias turned back to

William. "I found the entrance to where the Cryptoportal is, but I can't get through it."

"I can try," William said.

His grandfather forced himself to smile and glanced over at Goffman. The lift stopped and the door rolled to the side. "How long do we have until Abraham thaws?"

Goffman looked down at the cryo-counter. "Thirty-six minutes."

"Then we don't have any time to lose," Tobias said.

CHAPTER 29

The group moved through an underground hall deep inside the mountain. The walls were lined with tiny passageways and William wondered what it would have been like, back when people lived here.

"How long have you been down here?" William asked his grandfather as he walked next to him.

"I came here the instant Benjamin gave me the coordinates," he said, fiddling with the memory stick that was hanging around his neck. "We have known about the Cryptoportal for a long while," his grandfather continued, "but we thought that it had been destroyed."

"Are there more underground cities like this?" William asked, looking around.

"Yes," his grandfather said as if that went without saying. "They're all over the world, but there's only one portal."

They stopped in front of a small stone door that had strange symbols carved into it. William remembered what his grand-father had said about the myth: anyone who entered should expect never to return. He felt a slight tremble in his stomach.

"Why haven't I had any attacks yet?" he asked, looking up at grandfather.

"Now that the portal has been activated, it won't produce any more waves until Cornelia tries to send Abraham through it."

"And then?" William asked.

"Then you would suffer the most devastating attack," his grandfather said. "We have to stop her before she goes through with it." Tobias looked at Goffman. "How long now?"

Goffman looked at his watch. "Twenty-three minutes."

"We need to get going," Grandfather said and faced the stone door. "We have to get William down there to deactivate the portal."

"But how?" William said, at a loss. "How do I deactivate it?" He didn't like the feeling of being responsible for the fate of the entire planet.

"As far as I know," Tobias said, "the only thing that can control the Cryptoportal is the orb that Cornelia has. Somehow or other, you're going to have to get it from her. Now, come and help me solve this door. It'll be faster with two of us."

Tobias started moving the separate parts of the door and William followed his every move as he started to feel the tin-gling of the luridium in his stomach. His grandfather really was an excellent code-breaker.

"GET DOWN," Goffman suddenly yelled.

Instinctively, William threw himself to the ground as a beam hit the wall right above his head and turned it to dust. William looked back: Cornelia was coming towards them. The chauffeurs fired their passivators, but the rays hit an invisible shield in front of her. Cornelia barely flinched.

"That damned hand of hers," Tobias said, continuing to work on the door, but then another beam hit the wall and he disappeared in a cloud of dust. William heard him yell in agony.

"Grandad?" William shouted.

"Over here, William!" he shouted back.

William crawled over to the door and found his grandfather sitting up against the wall, clutching his leg.

"You have to solve the door," Tobias said, his face twisted in pain.

William got to his feet. He could hear the zapping of lasers and passivators and the shouts from Goffman and the others. It sounded like a full-fledged war was going on behind him and Cornelia was at the centre of it. He *had* to concentrate if he was to solve the code and get his grandfather to safety. William placed his hands on the door and the vibrations started in his stomach. He could already sense that, though this was a difficult code, it was within his reach ... he just didn't know if he could do it in time.

"Hurry," he heard his grandfather moan.

William watched the symbols lighting up and moved the pieces around on the door. As one symbol after the other fell into the right place, the door clicked from deep inside, then the last piece snapped into place and the door slid open.

"I did it!" William cried out.

He grabbed his grandfather by the arm and helped him through the door just as an avalanche of rocks fell from the roof of the cave, sending them tumbling down a narrow staircase.

CHAPTER 30

It was the sound that William noticed first. A strange mixture of deep rumbling and higher notes, sort of like incoherent music. He looked to the side and saw his grandfather on the floor next to him, covered in grey dust.

"Grandfather?" William said and crawled over to him.

"I'm OK," Tobias said, opening his eyes and forcing a smile. "I've been through worse. Can you give me a hand?"

William helped his grandfather to his feet and they both looked up at the staircase in front of them that was blocked by a mountain of large stones.

"The others are up there on the other side," William said.

"We can't afford to wait for them," his grandfather said. "I just hope they can keep Cornelia busy until we find the portal."

He motioned for William to follow and limped on. As William's eyes adjusted, he saw that everything around them was completely white – so white that it was hard to see where the walls ended and the ceiling began. The floor didn't make a single sound as they walked over it. William stomped a little harder to make sure, but it was as if the ground sucked all the sound away from his feet.

"How can this be many millions of years old and look like a–a spaceship from the future?" William stammered.

His grandfather didn't answer. They turned a corner and stopped.

"The portal must be behind that," Tobias said, pointing to a gigantic white door at the end of the room. "This is as far as I've managed to get."

William looked at the door. It was every bit as white as the walls, but it pulsed with a bluish light. "It doesn't have any symbols on it," William commented, "or a handle … or any way to open it."

"You have to use that," his grandfather said, pointing to something next to the door.

William's eyes widened – it was a massive robot that was so white it almost completely blended into the wall. It was similar to the one Iscia had shown him down at the Depository at the Institute, only this one was even bigger.

"It's an exoskeleton," his grandfather said. "It works with the same principles as the one your father has. We have found several of these around the world, and we have copied and developed the technology further, but this is still pretty advanced stuff."

"There's one like it at the Depository," William said.

"Yes, that's right," his grandfather said.

William walked over to the exoskeleton. He raised his hand and set it down on the enormous, white metal foot. It was cold to the touch. A ladder continued all the way up the leg and under a round indentation in the middle of the robot's chest and William could see a seat inside the hole.

"You want me to go up there?" he said, pointing.

Tobias nodded. "I went up there myself and checked it out, but I couldn't get anywhere."

William turned back to the exoskeleton again. He placed one foot on the bottom rung of the ladder and started climbing. The combination of the weird sounds in the room and the lofty height made him feel dizzy, but he continued upwards, concentrating on each step – it wasn't far now.

By the time William finally sat down in the white seat, sweat was pouring from his forehead. The seat was made of metal as well, but it was comfortable to sit in and felt as if it were made for him.

"Now what?" he called down to his grandfather, who was standing far down below, looking up at him.

"Put your hands on the plates. There's one on either side of you," his grandfather called back.

William spotted a white glass surface on both sides of the chair's armrests. He positioned one hand on the plate and then the other. His hands sank down as the glass reconfigured around his fingers.

"Try moving the arms," he heard his grandfather yell.

William moved his right hand, and the large robot arm did the same. He tried the other hand, with the same result.

"Put your feet on the plates on the floor," his grandfather instructed.

William looked down at two glass plates on the floor in front of him. He put one foot on each, and his feet sank down into the material.

"Now you can make it walk."

William moved his feet and the large exoskeleton did the same.

"Take a couple steps towards me." His grandfather waved William over with both hands.

William moved one foot in front of the other. The large metal construction jerked as it began to walk. He took a couple of steps, then stopped.

"Good. You've got the hang of it," his grandfather called out. "Now walk over to the door."

William turned the large exoskeleton and walked over to the white door, which was still pulsing with a faint, blue light. He raised the robot's hands, splayed the fingers and then placed them against the door. The surface immediately glowed blue around the large robot hands and the high notes in the room altered.

"You need to use the notes to open the door," his grandfather said. "I've been trying for two days, but I can't solve it."

William looked at the massive robot hands in front of him. He moved one hand to another location on the white surface and the tone of the high notes in the room changed. *This is like playing a piano,* he thought.

"I think I need to make a melody to open the door," he called out.

"Get to it then," his grandfather responded. "We don't have much time."

William closed his eyes and concentrated. He felt the vibrations move up his spine and out into his arms and fingers. When he opened his eyes again, he saw lights in every colour of the rainbow dancing over the white door in front of him. He knew that the luridium was helping him to solve the code and he mimicked the movements of the colours, pressing each one with the robotic hands. At first, there was no coherence to the sound, but then a melody emerged.

He played the notes, working his hands faster and faster as the melody became stronger. Then the lights vanished and the music faded away. There was a deep rumble and the large white door moved downwards into the floor. William took a couple of steps back with the exoskeleton and watched as the opening revealed a dark hallway on the other side.

CHAPTER 31

"We have to get in there," Tobias yelled and limped towards the opening.

"What about the others?" William protested.

"We don't have time," his grandfather said and continued.

William climbed down the ladder on the side of the exoskeleton's leg and jumped off the last rung. He caught up with his grandfather – who was badly limping now – as he turned on the little lamp on the top of his passivator and lit up the surroundings.

"How's your leg?" William asked in a low voice.

"Fine," Tobias said through gritted teeth. He swung the beam of light back and forth over the darkness ahead of them.

"Do you know how to get to the portal?" William asked.

"No … but now that we're through the gate," his grandfather said, "it shouldn't be hard to find."

Suddenly, William heard something … a dizzying, deep rumble that made the floor tremble.

"What's that noise?" William asked.

"It's the portal," his grandfather said and pointed the lamp into the darkness ahead. "Wait … there's something there," he whispered.

Two stone robots stood motionless at the end of the hallway, like sculptures covered in dust. They looked like the exoskeleton William had just used, only these were smaller and granite-grey in colour.

"What are they?" William whispered back.

"Guards," Tobias said without taking his eyes off the robots. "If something happens, I'll try to distract them while you get to the portal."

Tobias kept his passivator aimed at the robots as they moved towards them.

"Maybe they're inactive?" William said.

"Let's hope so," his grandfather said, his voice trembling. "If they haven't moved by now then I doubt—"

In an instant, both robots straightened up and came at them, swirling dust into the air. Tobias fired the passivators and the rays hit one of the machines, causing it to stagger backwards for a moment before regaining its balance.

"Run!" Tobias yelled, pushing the passivator into William's hands. "I'll only slow you down."

"But—" William said.

"RUN! Now! You have to find the portal and stop Cornelia!"

Tobias limped back the way they had come in as the two robots clanked after him. William turned and ran as fast as his legs would carry him – speeding past an almost endless network of hallways on either side of him. But, after a while, adrenaline started to make every muscle in his body shake. He stopped and tried to quiet his breathing.

The noise was much louder now – a low bass boomed from the floor and walls and made his vision blurry. William held the heavy passivator up and followed the sound. He turned a corner and stopped. He was standing in an enormous hall made of seemingly endless stone walls and a vaulted ceiling high above. He recognized the large golden ring that hovered in the middle of the hall immediately, although it was impossible to tell exactly how big it was, and it was so bright that it almost hurt to look at it.

Gentle vibrations started in his stomach – it felt like the luridium was starting to move inside him. William looked up at the hovering ring again. He felt as if it were calling to him … wanting him to come closer.

He lowered his gaze and noticed the white rectangular chest on the ground. It was Abraham Talley's cryogenic freezer unit.

CHAPTER 32

There was a series of red blinking numbers on the display on the side of the freezer unit. The display showed 00:10:08, but the numbers were quickly changing – counting down to just over ten minutes' time when Abraham would be thawed.

William's heart hammered in his chest and a paralyzing fear spread through his body. He looked up at the hovering ring and thought about those beings – full of luridium – that had left Earth all those years ago. Was that why he felt attracted to the portal? Was the luridium in him trying to entice him to leave the planet too? The idea felt strangely compelling and, all of a sudden, William wondered whether he should stop fighting and let himself be sent away.

"You feel it, don't you?" Cornelia said from behind him.

William whipped around, but there was no one there.

"Did your precious grandfather leave you in the lurch?" Cornelia asked. "And not for the first time, right? He's deserted you before, hasn't he?"

William raised the passivator and tried to ignore her words.

"No matter what they tricked you into believing, William, you don't belong with them. You're a machine, not a human."

"I'M NOT A MACHINE!" he yelled.

"Stop lying to yourself, William. You're different. You're not like the others."

"NO!" William shouted back.

"Remember, if you ever want to see your little friend again," Cornelia said, "you'll do as I say."

"Where is she?"

William turned around and saw Cornelia standing a couple of metres away, watching him with her wild eyes and her leather bag in one hand.

"Let me see her!" William shouted and pointed his passivator at Cornelia.

Cornelia looked over at Abraham's freezer. "Eight minutes left." She grinned. "We might as well have a little fun while we wait."

She pushed various buttons on her mechanical hand and pointed it into the middle of the room. A beam of light shot out and the contours of a person began to materialize. Soon Iscia was suspended in the air a little way ahead of them. Her eyes were closed and her head lolled to the side.

"Iscia!" William yelled.

"There's no point in shouting. She can't hear you."

"Show me that she's alive," William shouted and pointed the passivator at Abraham's freezer. There was a glint of surprise in Cornelia's eyes.

"OK," she said. "I'll play along for a few minutes."

Cornelia aimed her mechanical hand at Iscia and shot out a ray that that made her body jerk into life.

"Iscia!" William called out.

Iscia looked around the room with frightened eyes. He wanted to run to her, but Cornelia seemed to know what he was thinking.

"Stay still," Cornelia screamed. "It will soon be time." She looked at the display on Abraham's freezer. "Now, your pretty little girlfriend can watch as you make yourself useful."

"What's going on?" Iscia asked, her voice trembling.

"Open the lid on the freezer!" Cornelia commanded and aimed her mechanical hand at Iscia.

"Don't do it!" Iscia said. "You know what will happen if he makes it through."

With a loud *zap* Cornelia fired a blue beam that hit Iscia, who instantly fell to the floor.

"No!" William yelled.

Iscia moaned and grabbed her head.

"Next time I'll give her a lethal dose," Cornelia said. "Open the lid!"

William had no choice. He walked over to the freezer unit, his whole body bristling at the thought of what he had to do.

"Turn the handle." Cornelia ordered.

William raised his hand and put it on the chrome handle on the top of the lid. He glanced back at Iscia, then slowly turned the handle to the side. There was a loud *fsssssssst* … as if the whole freezer were inhaling. William took a couple of steps back, without taking his eyes off the unit. The lid tipped open and a frosty mist poured out of the box. A blue light blinked to life and, through the smoke, William could make out the contours of a motionless body inside the unit. Abraham's body.

Tears poured down Iscia's cheeks and William knew that she would never forgive him – even if he was doing it to save her.

"Now what?" he said turning to Cornelia.

"Move away," Cornelia said. "It will be my honour to do the rest."

She came towards him, unzipping the leather bag. The little cockroach crawled out, scurried across her arm and took refuge in one of her jacket pockets. Cornelia took out the orb and placed it on a round metallic plate set into the floor. The instant the orb hit the brass, the large metallic ring above them began to spin and a bright beam of light shot out from it down to the freezer. Cornelia took a couple of steps backwards, her eyes fixed on Abraham's glowing body as it levitated towards the spinning ring.

William had to fight the urge to just walk into the portal and let it carry him away. The ring was vibrating powerfully now and the floor shook under him. He felt the cold creeping up his spine and knew that an attack was on its way. Soon he would lose control of his body and everything would be over.

CHAPTER 33

The cold poured through William's body as he watched Abraham travel towards the beam of light. Then the rumbling in his stomach increased and abdominal cramps hit him like a hard fist to the gut. His legs turned to jelly and William dropped to the ground, writhing in agony. He gritted his teeth and, with agonizing effort, lifted his head and looked at Iscia, who had slumped back down on the floor. He tried calling out to her, but his mouth wouldn't cooperate.

Cornelia stood with her back to him, gazing at Abraham's body, which was now halfway to the portal. Cornelia had won and William was struggling to fight the desire to close his eyes and let the seizure carry him away.

There was a movement inside one of Cornelia's jacket pockets and the cockroach crawled out – its antennas fluttering in the air like two little swords. And just like that, an idea materialized in William's mind. He remembered what Benjamin had told him in the lab; there was enough luridium inside the cockroach to enhance William's abilities, but there would be no way of knowing whether he would become a machine, or whether he would keep some of his human qualities.

William felt his whole body relax like it knew that he had already made a decision. It was his only chance now. He struggled into a sitting position and stayed there for a few seconds looking at the cockroach standing on the edge of Cornelia's pocket. William glanced at Iscia – her eyes were frightened and wide and she shook her head. It was like she knew what he was planning to do, and how dangerous it was.

William suddenly felt an intense anger growing inside him. He couldn't let Cornelia and Abraham win. He would do everything in his power to prevent them from succeeding – even if it meant sacrificing himself. He fought his way onto his knees – the pain was unbearable but he forced himself up and staggered towards Cornelia. Her full attention was on Abraham – it was only a matter of seconds before he would enter the portal ring. William stopped right behind her.

Iscia sat up and William put his index finger to his mouth, signalling for her to keep quiet. Carefully, he reached out towards the cockroach At first, it didn't seem to notice him, then William felt his heart jump as he realized that the cockroach was also having a seizure. He quickly snatched the insect and ran away. It vibrated powerfully now, struggling to get free, but William clutched it in his fist.

Cornelia whipped around. "What are you doing, you little brat?" she barked. "Give it back now!"

"No," William said, shaking his head.

"I said, GIVE IT BACK!" Cornelia screamed.

His paralysing pain was replaced with an intense anger. Why should he let Cornelia tell him what to do? Why should he have to choose between Iscia and the world? He didn't care what happened to him any more, all that mattered was to get Iscia to safety and stop Cornelia from sending Abraham through the portal.

Cornelia raised her mechanical hand and pointed it at William, but she hesitated. Was the cockroach that important to her? William opened his fist and looked at it. It had stopped shaking, and lay completely still now.

"Give … it … to … me," Cornelia said, her voice trembling with anger.

William ignored her, and continued to back away, keeping his full attention on it. Tiny silvery droplets appeared on the cockroach's shell, as though it was sweating metal. The droplets were attracted to each other, like liquid magnets that clumped together to form even larger drops. This was exactly what William had hoped for – the luridium was leaving the insect, attracted by the larger amounts of luridium inside William's body. The metal rolled from the beetle and into his palm before disappearing through the pores of his skin. And like that, it was gone.

William looked up at Cornelia, who stood there staring at him. It was as if time had stopped, then he started shaking uncontrollably as a surge of energy shot through his body. The luridium from the cockroach was merging with his own luridium. He looked down at the insect, which jumped from his hand onto the floor and scrambled towards Cornelia.

William knew what he had to do. He shot towards the orb under the golden ring. He could hear Cornelia screaming, but her voice sounded muffled and far away. She was coming towards him, but seemed to be running in slow motion, like she was underwater. William looked up at Abraham, who had almost reached the ring. He bent down and grabbed the orb from its place.

The moment he removed the orb, Abraham's suspended body stopped moving and the golden ring stopped spinning. William walked backwards, holding the orb in his hands. He realized he had gained control over his attack. Maybe it was from the extra amounts of luridium he had absorbed, but he felt stronger and more focused than ever.

William turned around just in time to see Cornelia fling herself at him – her face contorted in rage. He fell backwards, still clutching the orb with both hands as he landed hard on his back with Cornelia on top of him. In an instant, time returned to normal.

"Give me that!" she yelled, baring her yellow teeth and stinging his eyes with her rancid breath. Cornelia aimed her mechanical hand right at his head. William suddenly remembered how the hand had moved around by itself on the plane, and how Cornelia had twisted it back in place. He quickly set the orb down and grabbed the hand. It beeped louder and louder, charging for a powerful blast – he was about to be melted into the floor, just like poor old Pontus. He took a firm grip and twisted it in one direction then in the opposite direction. With a quiet *click* the whole hand came off.

"NOOOOOO!" Cornelia screamed, reaching for it with her other hand as William quickly scrambled to his feet. "GIVE IT BACK!" she cried, rushing at him.

William stood his ground, aimed the hand at her and pushed all the buttons at the same time. There was a loud *zap* and a light ray shot out, grazing Cornelia's coat.

"How do you know how to do that?" she hissed.

He pressed the buttons again. Another beam shot out of the hand and hit her square in the stomach, sending her flying across the floor. William stood there waiting for her to get back up and attack him, but she didn't move. As he stepped closer, he could see that half her body was melted into the ground. Cornelia's eyes were closed and her head was tilted forward.

The portal started vibrating again. William looked around and saw Freddy standing by the freezer. Somehow the orb was back in its place on the floor and Abraham's body was ascending towards the spinning ring again.

"Freddy?" William shouted. "What are you doing?"

"She's in my head… she's making me do these things," he shouted. "Please make her stop!"

"What are you talking about?" William shouted. "Make who stop?"

"I'm sorry, William," Freddy said, his eyes red from tears. "She made me trick you in the Depository…"

"It's too late!" Iscia suddenly shouted. "Look!"

Abraham's glowing body entered through the spinning ring, and then he was gone. William couldn't believe it. They had lost.

"William," he heard Iscia shout from behind him. "It's Freddy! Stop him!"

Freddy was walking towards the beam of light under the portal.

"STOP!" William shouted. "STOP!"

But Freddy didn't respond and kept moving forwards.

"FREDDY!" William yelled and started after him. "What are you doing?"

Freddy stopped and looked at Iscia. "I'm sorry," he said before stepping into the light. His body jerked violently, and then went limp. He fell backwards into a horizontal position and floated towards the ring.

"Stop him!" Iscia yelled as Freddy started to ascend along the beam like Abraham had done.

William grabbed hold of Freddy's leg, but the force pulling Freddy towards the portal was so strong that he couldn't hold on. William lost his grip and watched in horror as Freddy's body disappeared into the golden ring.

In an instant, William knew he only had one option left. He had to deactivate the portal before anyone else went through it, or, worse, came back from the other side. He quickly bent down and picked up the orb. The beam of light disappeared and everything went quiet as he held the orb in his hands. Vibrations shot up his spine and out into his arms and the ancient symbols on the orb lit up and exploded into the air. They swirled around him like a school of fish then broke apart into smaller groups. Some of the symbols were smaller, but others were much bigger. They sped around him and crashed into other symbols, forming new ones in small explosions. Different colours flashed in front of his eyes and William knew which symbols to follow with his gaze.

His hands started moving very fast – faster than they had ever moved before. He looked down as his feet suddenly left the foor. His mind flashed back to what happened in the Depository – he knew he would have to work quickly, otherwise he would float higher and higher. His hands turned and twisted the old orb unbelievably fast. The parts were hard to move at first, but they quickly eased up and became more cooperative. Was the extra boost of luridium in his body speeding up his reactions? It had to be.

In a moment, he had solved the orb, but his hands kept moving. He had found a secret mode and somehow he knew it would destroy the portal for good. As soon as the last piece of the code was entered, the huge ring stopped spinning, the golden light faded away and, with a thunderous bang, the portal fell to the ground making the whole hall shake.

William dropped to the floor and everything went black.

CHAPTER 34

William ran to Iscia and helped her to her feet. "Can you walk?"

"I think so," she said.

Her legs wobbled as William supported her and they hurried away from the wrecked portal.

"Is it over?" Iscia asked as William helped her sit up against the wall.

"I think so," William said. He looked over at the ring then at Cornelia's body sticking out of the stone floor.

"Is she dead?" Iscia asked.

"I don't know," William said as he looked at Cornelia's mechanical hand lying on the ground not far from her. Footsteps sounded behind him as Goffman raced into the room, covered in sweat and dust.

"What happened?" he asked with a trembling voice. "Where's Abraham?" Goffman looked at William, who shook his head.

"And Freddy? He ran ahead of us…"

William was about to answer, but stopped as his grandfather came into the room. He spotted William and limped over to him.

"Are you two OK?" he asked.

William nodded. "But Abraham…" William started.

"You did so well," his grandfather said, looking at the ring lying on the ground. "They won't be able to come back using that anyway."

He gazed at William with proud eyes. He was about to say more when something behind him caught William's attention.

Cornelia was moving. Her right arm reached out for something.

The mechanical hand.

Before William knew it, he was on his feet running towards her as she grabbed her mechanical hand, turned it and pointed it at him. There was a bright flash of light, but the beam missed him and he raced on – he had to get to her before she could fire it again.

Then, she did something completely unexpected. She turned the hand on herself … and fired. With a flash of light, she was gone. All that was left was the mechanical hand, which dropped to the floor with a loud *clank*. William skidded to a halt, looking in disbelief at the empty hole in the ground before him.

"William!" Iscia cried.

He turned. His heart dropped as he saw his grandfather

lying on the ground next to Iscia.

"The beam…" Iscia called out. "It hit him…"

"No…" William screamed as he ran back. He threw himself to his knees and held his grandfather's head in his hands. His grandfather's body was becoming transparent.

"Please, no…" he cried out.

"William," his grandfather whispered, opening his hand to reveal a memory stick attached to a chain. "Take it. Hang it around your neck. It's yours now."

William pulled the chain over his head without taking his eyes off his grandfather.

"I'm sorry." William was sobbing now.

"You're going to have to manage without me now," his grandfather said, smiling. "You have to continue the work I started, and do everything in your power to stop Abraham from coming back."

"But how?" William whispered. "I don't know how…" He had so many questions he still wanted to ask his grandfather – so many things he wanted to talk to him about – but he didn't know what to say or do.

"The Institute will help you…" his grandfather said.

William sat there stunned. He knew there was nothing he could do to save him and tears flowed down his cheeks as he watched his grandfather's face grow paler. He held his head and realized that he could see his own fingers through his grandfather's forehead.

"Never forget how much I love you, William," he said, "and how proud I am of you."

William felt his grandfather almost disintegrate in his hands, like fine sand slipping through his fingers. The more he tried to hold on to him, the faster it seemed to happen.

"Grandad…" he sobbed in anguish. "Don't leave me … please…"

William stared at the floor where his grandfather had been lying. He couldn't believe what had happened. His grandfather was gone.

CHAPTER 35

William sat up and opened his eyes. His face was covered in sweat and his breathing was laboured. It felt like he had just sprinted up a hill, but he hadn't. As he looked around and took in his surroundings, he saw that he was on an aeroplane, surrounded by people. It took another couple of seconds before he realized that he wasn't in danger any more.

He sat back and recalled the trek down the mountains with Iscia, Goffman and the two chauffeurs. Then the quiet car journey as Goffman had taken William and Iscia to the airport and booked them on a commercial flight back to England. And then there was what had happened in the cave. Freddy... his grandfather. With a heavy feeling in his stomach, he went over every detail. It was as though an invisible force had pulled Freddy into the portal – and he still couldn't quite make sense of Cornelia shooting his grandfather. He wondered if there was anything more he could have done to save them both.

He looked down at his hands. He had managed to overcome his attacks, and he had survived absorbing more luridium. The portal had been destroyed and Abraham would not be able to use it to come back again. But his grandfather was dead. Freddy was surely dead. Everything that he had done to save the world was dwarfed by a huge dark cloud that hung over him. It was like a bad dream that he couldn't wake up from.

"This is your captain," said a voice over the speakers. "We have started our descent towards London, and will be on the ground in approximately twenty minutes."

"Finally," said a voice over him. "You're awake."

William looked up and saw Iscia standing in the aisle next to him. She squeezed past him and dropped into her seat. She had a small bag of nuts in one hand and a carton of apple juice in the other.

"Thought you would be hungry when you woke up," she said and held up the bag and the carton. "You've slept non-stop for eleven hours."

"Thanks," William said and took the carton, opening it and gulping down the sweet liquid. Then, he took the bag of nuts. He was starving. He could feel the nuts pressing towards the inside of his cheeks as he chewed. He must have looked funny, because Iscia giggled.

William swallowed and placed the empty bag and carton in the seat pocket in front of him. It felt like he had slept for years. Suddenly he remembered the flash drive his grandfather had given him. He grabbed at his chest but found nothing. The chain was gone. He was hit by a sudden wave of panic.

"I put it in your pocket," Iscia said reassuringly and pointed at his jacket. "You tried to pull it off in your sleep – I was afraid you would snap the chain."

William thrust his hand into his jacket pocket and felt the small flash drive. He relaxed a little and slipped it over his head and around his neck again.

They sat for a while in silence.

"I just can't believe it," William mumbled. "He's gone…"

"I know," she said and leaned back in her seat. "It doesn't feel real – I'm not sure it ever will. The thought that he could actually die never even occurred to me."

"Yeah," William said quietly.

He looked down at the flash drive. "Wonder what's on it," he said, wanting to change the subject. It was too painful talking about his grandfather in the past tense.

"We'll find out soon enough," Iscia said.

"I'm sorry about Freddy… do you think he could have survived going through the portal?" William asked and looked at Iscia.

Her face became stiff and pale, and she lowered her gaze.

"I don't know… I just don't understand what came over him," she whispered. "It was like someone made him do it."

"Just before he went into the portal, he apologized for making me solving the orb in the Depository … I think that somehow she was controlling him all along. Do you think he's with Abraham right now?"

"I hope not," Iscia said. "But then again, if he is, at least that means he's alive."

William looked out of the window again. "I have a strange feeling we're going to see him again at some point. Are you going back?" William asked, "to the Institute?"

"It's my home," she said with a flat smile. "I don't have anywhere else to go."

"Why?" William asked. He felt bad for not knowing the answer.

"I'll tell you someday," Iscia said and turned her head to look out of the window. "What about you? Are you coming back?"

"I don't know," William said and scratched his head. "Now that my grandfather…"

William stopped talking. He sat for a while deep in thought. Maybe the Institute didn't want him back after what he had done at the Depository for Impossible Archaeology. He'd also failed to prevent Cornelia sending Abraham and Freddy through the Cryptoportal. He didn't exactly feel like a hero.

"I think they need you more than ever," Iscia said and gave him a reassuring smile. It was as if she had read his mind.

"Maybe," he said.

Then she became serious. "Were you really going to go

through with it?" she asked in a near whisper, as if she didn't want anyone to hear.

"With what?" William asked, even though he knew what she was talking about.

"Helping Cornelia send him through the portal?"

William didn't know what to say.

"The whole earth is more important than me," she whispered.

"I know," he said, but deep down he wasn't sure that he meant it. To him, Iscia was becoming one of the most important people in the entire universe.

Iscia gazed at him. She was about to say something when the voice of a little girl interrupted her.

"I know who you are," the voice said.

William looked up and saw a girl's head sticking over the seat in front of them.

"Huh?" he said, confused.

"I know who you are," the girl said once more. "I've seen you on TV."

It dawned on William what the girl was talking about and his chest started tightening up. She had probably seen him on TV when he'd lost against Vektor Hansen.

"You're William Wenton," the girl said, "the world's greatest code-breaker." The girl held up something William recognized immediately: the Difficulty. The toy puzzle William hadn't managed to solve during the TV show.

William stared at the plastic cylinder. A wave of bad memories washed over him: his first attack, Vektor Hansen's gloating, the fear and insecurity.

"Where did you get that?" William asked.

The girl looked at William like he had dropped down from the sky.

"At the toy shop of course," she said. "Everyone has one."

William looked around the plane. Many of the passengers were looking at him now and some stuck their heads together and whispered.

"I've been trying for days now," someone said behind him.

William turned his head and saw a little boy standing in the aisle next to him. He was also holding the Difficulty. "It's almost impossible to solve it."

"Yeah, it's hard," a man in a suit said from a couple of seats away. He held up the toy and smiled.

"It seems like everyone really does have one," Iscia whispered as she looked around the cabin.

"Can you solve mine?" the girl in front of William asked and held up her puzzle.

"Er…" William hesitated.

"Please," the girl said.

"Come on," said the boy in the aisle.

William could feel his stomach tensing. Yes, it reminded him of that fatal TV appearance, but back then, he didn't know what was behind his seizures. Now he had taken care of that problem. He looked down at the Difficulty again and thought of something. This stupid toy was the only code he hadn't managed to solve. Ever. William looked at Iscia.

"Wouldn't hurt…" She shrugged her shoulders and smiled.

William could feel his pulse go up. His body tingled.

"OK," he said.

The little girl placed the Difficulty in his hand. William leaned back in his seat and looked at the plastic cylinder. All eyes were on him and an eerie silence fell over the cabin.

He closed his eyes. The vibrations began immediately and, like always, they started in his stomach, then travelled up his spine and out into his arms. Everything around him faded away, and soon, the only thing he could see was the Difficulty.

The vibrations continued out into his hands and stopped. William couldn't feel anything for a few seconds. For a moment, he thought that once again he would fail to solve that stupid toy. Then the vibrations came back with a vengeance and his fingers started to work, faster and faster. Time and place faded and William was lost in deep concentration.

The Difficulty was suddenly yanked from his hands. William came around and looked at the floor. Had he dropped it like he did at the TV show?

Then he heard it: applause and cheering. Most of the people surrounding him had their arms in the air and big grins on their faces. He looked over at Iscia, who smiled and patted him on the back. The little girl who had given him the Difficulty held it in the air and shouted.

"HE DID IT… I KNEW HE WOULD DO IT!"

William looked at the toy. The little girl was right! The cylinder had split into two pieces.

"And you set a new world record," the boy next to him said enthusiastically. He looked down at the mobile phone he held in his hand. "Thirteen seconds. Vektor Hansen's old record was more than a minute."

Even though it was just a plastic toy, William had never been so relived to solve a code. William Wenton, the world-famous code-breaker was back to his old self.

CHAPTER 36

William stopped in the door to his room. He'd only been home for two hours – before that he had spent a couple of days at the Institute for debriefing, and they had a formal ceremony marking his grandfather's passing. As soon as he had arrived home, William's mother had spent most of the time hugging him and feeding him pancakes, while his father wanted to know everything about what had happened. They were both distraught by his grandfather's passing but, equally, they were relieved to have William back home safely.

Even if it had been just a couple of weeks since he was here last it felt like years had passed. He was different from the person he'd been when he last had been here. He was somehow stronger. William's gaze stopped at the old desk his grandfather had given him. He put his hand on the cool wood and stroked the strange marks and symbols on the surface that Tobias had carved into it many years ago. Then he looked at a newspaper that his mother had put on the desk. He read the front page: *The difficulty new record: 13 seconds. William Wenton may be a genius after all. Vektor Hansen claims foul play and demands rematch.*

William folded it up, put it inside one of the desk drawers and sat on the chair.

His flipped the lid of his laptop open and grabbed the flash drive that still hung on a chain around his neck. He had wanted to wait until he was alone to see what his grandfather had left for him. He placed it in the USB-port on the side of the computer and waited. His foot shook up and down in excitement while he stared in anticipation at the screen. But nothing happened – it didn't even seem like the computer had registered the drive. He could feel the disappointment creep over him. He had hoped that there would be something on it that would make him feel better. A message from his grandfather, perhaps even a video message.

He removed the drive from the USB-slot and waited a little before re-inserting it. Still nothing. William slammed the laptop shut in frustration and got up from the chair. He turned and headed for the door.

"Where are you going?" a voice said from behind him.

William stopped.

"You have to be a little bit more patient," the voice said. It somehow sounded familiar to him and he slowly turned around. He couldn't see anyone in the room.

"Come back here," the voice said.

William looked at the laptop. It couldn't be.

"What are you waiting for?" the voice said.

It felt like an electric shock shot through William's body. It couldn't be. That would be … impossible. He opened the laptop. At first the screen was completely blank, then a familiar face appeared.

"You look startled," Tobias Wenton said and smiled up at him.

"I… I…" William stammered. He was so surprised that his mouth had stopped working.

"Can you hear me?" his grandfather said.

William nodded his head.

"Good," Tobias said. "I was starting to worry that the software had failed me."

"Software?" William said.

"Yes. My software."

"Yours?" William was confused now. "What are you?"

"I'm me," Tobias said.

"But how… You … you died," William said. It was weird saying it out loud.

Grandfather looked a little gloomy, like he hadn't known.

"You can tell me how that happened later … I must have given you the flash drive then?"

William couldn't do anything but nod.

"I've spent the last year digitalizing my brain," his grandfather explained.

"Does that mean that it's really you inside there?" William said.

"Of course," he said. "Up until the moment I stopped backing the data up, which must have been about a week ago."

William stared at his grandfather's face. It was like having a video conversation with him.

"So you're not really dead?" William said.

"Correct. It's still me. I just don't have a body ... yet." Tobias smiled. William did too. "Anyway, I'm sure that you and the Institute could do with my help for a little while longer?"

"Yes," William said and laughed.

William needed his grandfather more than ever. He was his family, but he was also his all-time hero.

DON'T MISS THE FIRST WILLIAM WENTON ADVENTURE!

When his extraordinary talent for codebreaking
is discovered, William Wenton is taken to
the Institute for Post-Human Research.

But someone is after him and will stop at nothing to
find William and use his special skills to unearth a
strange and powerful substance called luridium.

"William Wenton cracks the code for great adventure.
Mystery, action, a great hero and fantastic robots —
what more could you ask for?"
Shane Hegarty, author of *Darkmouth*

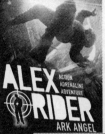
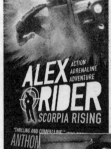

Bobbie Peers is an award-winning Norwegian film director and scriptwriter who studied at The London Film School. Peers made his début as a writer for children in 2015 with *Luridiumstyven*, published for the first time in English as *William Wenton and the Luridium Thief*. This first, thrilling adventure featuring the codebreaking whizz William, won the Ark Children's Award and the Children's Book Award in its native Norway and was shortlisted for the Bokslukerprisen. The book has now been translated into over thirty different languages and is set to become a feature film.